"You walk around, your head in the clouds."

Lucius laughed softly. "Why do you think of yourself as a staid old woman who'll never see forty again? You're twenty-seven and you look ten years younger. And I'm not paying compliments — I know you too well for that."

"What are you going to do?" asked Katrina, not liking the sound of that laugh.

"Do? Why call your sister's bluff. I shall turn my attentions to you, Katie. In due course we shall become engaged, and when you've had time to gather together whatever it is that girls gather together before they marry, we'll be wed. Here in Upper Tew."

For a big man he was very fast on his feet. Before she could gather her wits to answer he had left her, closing the door very quietly behind him.

HARLEQUIN ROMANCES
by Betty Neels

These books may be available at your local bookseller.

For a free catalog listing all titles currently available,
send your name and address to:

Harlequin Reader Service
P.O. Box 52040, Phoenix, AZ 85072-9988
Canadian address: Stratford, Ontario N5A 6W2

Roses and Champagne

Betty Neels

Harlequin Books

TORONTO • NEW YORK • LONDON
AMSTERDAM • PARIS • SYDNEY • HAMBURG
STOCKHOLM • ATHENS • TOKYO • MILAN

Original hardcover edition published in 1983
by Mills & Boon Limited

ISBN 0-373-02597-1

Harlequin Romance first edition January 1984

CHAPTER ONE

THE wintry sun, shining in through the wide windows, gave the room a false warmth, for there was no fire in the handsome steel grate and there was a decided chill in the air; a chilliness strongly echoed by the two people in the room, facing each other across the handsome Soumak carpet, a young woman with pale brown hair and beautiful brown eyes in an unremarkable face, sitting very upright in a Victorian balloon chair, and a man in his thirties, dark-haired, grey-eyed and with a high-bridged nose which didn't detract from his good looks. He was a tall, well built man and the armchair he was leaning against creaked as he folded his arms along its back.

'What a silly girl you're being, Katrina,' he observed in a voice tinged with impatience. 'Anyone would think that it was you whose heart had been broken!' He grinned at her and she made a small indignant sound.

'I can find no possible excuse for you . . .' she began. She had a nice quiet voice, waspish at the moment though.

'My dear girl, I'm flattered that you should try to find excuses for me.'

She shot him a furious look, her black brows drawn together in a frown.

'Don't be ridiculous,' she begged crossly. 'It's the last thing I'd do. You've broken Virginia's heart . . .'

He came round the chair and sat down,

5

stretching out his long legs in comfort. 'Now who's being ridiculous?' he wanted to know. 'Virginia hasn't got a heart. From the moment she could toddle you know as well as I do that she made a point of twisting everyone round her thumb. She did it charmingly too.' He eyed her thoughtfully. 'You never did that, Katrina.'

'Much good it would have done me.' She was matter-of-fact about it. And then, her voice cold with anger again: 'She's in her room, crying . . .'

She was interrupted: 'Of course she's crying—spoilt girls who can't have their own way always cry. She'll stop presently.'

'You're heartless, Lucius.' Her eyes searched his face and saw nothing but mockery there. She got to her feet. 'Will you go away? I don't want to talk to you—there's nothing to say anyway.'

He sauntered to the door. 'Not while you're in this silly sentimental mood.' As he went through the door he said: 'I passed young Lovell on my way here, so Virginia had better repair that broken heart pretty quickly.'

'You're unspeakable!' declared Katrina, and heard him laugh as he shut the door.

She went to a window presently and watched him make his leisurely way across the lawn, taking the short cut to the side gate which would lead him to the stables where Gem, his mare, would be. It was a pity, she thought sadly, that they could no longer be friends. She had a sudden vivid memory of him, a ten-year-old schoolboy sitting his pony patiently holding the leading reins of her own fat Shetland. She had been three years old and Virginia wasn't even thought of . . .

And they had stayed friends, and even when Virginia, the spoilt darling of the family had made a threesome, they had neither of them minded; indeed, as the years passed, Lucius and Virginia spent more and more time together, naturally enough, for by then Katrina's talent for drawing and painting had got her a job illustrating children's books. Her father had had one of the attics turned into a studio for her and she had worked there contentedly, making a tolerable income for herself, although that was quite unnecessary. But she had been glad of it when her parents were killed in a car accident, for a good deal of money died with them and the pleasant quite large house and its several acres of ground absorbed a lot of the income which was left. All the same, she had contrived very well; Virginia had finished her expensive education, had all the clothes she wanted and ran her own small car. Now at twenty she was the darling of the neighbourhood, as pretty as a picture and taking it for granted that every man she met would fall in love with her. Which, more or less, they did. Katrina, a year earlier, used to Virginia's constant brief love affairs, but anxious that at nineteen she should turn her hand to something useful, had roped in Lucius. 'Look,' she had said, 'Virginia's got so many boy-friends she can't remember their names—I don't mind, it must be fun,' just for a moment she had sounded wistful and he had given her a long thoughtful look, 'but I wondered if she would train for something, meet older men perhaps. What do you think?'

That had been a year ago. He had laughed and agreed and said: 'I'm an older man, aren't I? She can start on me. What do you want me to interest her in? Book-keeping? Or how to run an estate?'

He hadn't done either, thought Katrina sadly,

although he was a chartered accountant and
Stockley House and its surrounding acres belonged
to him. Instead he had given Virginia her head,
whirled her up to London to dine and dance and
visit theatres, ridden with her almost every day,
and although he had never given her a ring, it was
a foregone conclusion that it was only a question
of Virginia making up her mind between emeralds
and rubies.

And now it was all over and Lucius was
behaving abominably. Katrina paused to think
here; according to Virginia he had behaved
abominably and he certainly showed no signs of
remorse about that, although she hadn't actually
asked him ... Well, what could she have said
anyway? Ever since she could remember, he had
retired behind an expressionless face if he didn't
want you to know something; he'd worn that face
this morning, and she hadn't dared probe too
deep. She sighed; they had known each other for
so long. The thought of not having his friendship
any more was depressing but what else could she
do? Virginia had screamed at her that she would
never speak to him again, and it was going to be
rather difficult if she was to continue the easy
companionship she had known for so long. And
she would be disloyal to Virginia too. She herself
was to blame anyway—encouraging Virginia to
spend so much of her time with Lucius; it was
inevitable that she should fall in love with him,
even more inevitable that he should fall in love
with her, or so one would have supposed. He had
certainly indulged Virginia in everything she
wanted to do or have, and then last night they had
come back from a dance at one of the local
houses. Katrina shuddered at the memory.

Virginia had been beside herself, her voice shrill and almost hysterical, declaring that she would kill him, kill herself, kill everyone ... her heart was broken, she would go into a convent, run away from home, throw herself in the river. She had sobbed and screamed into Katrina's dressing-gowned shoulder, and Lucius had stood just inside the door and laughed.

'I'll never forgive him!' declared Katrina to the empty room.

The door opened and she turned round to face Mrs Beecham's rosy round face. 'Will Mr Lucius be staying to lunch?' asked that lady, and at Katrina's forceful no, nodded her head. 'I thought perhaps he wouldn't be, and that's a great pity, because there's to be a cheese soufflé and mushrooms—he brought 'em over himself, picked 'em this morning.'

'No mushrooms,' declared Katrina fiercely; she loved them, but it smacked of giving in to the enemy, 'and he's not staying, Mrs Beecham.'

'Just as well, maybe, Miss Katrina, because there's Miss Virginia carrying on something shocking up in her room—won't let Maudie in to clean neither.'

'I'll go up,' said Katrina, and went out of the room, crossed the polished floor of the wide hall and went up the uncarpeted stairs, the treads worn from the countless feet which had used them over a couple of centuries. The landing above was wide as the hall and several doors opened from it. She could hear her sister's voice as she turned the handle and went into a room in the front of the house.

Virginia was sitting up in bed, an untouched breakfast tray on the table beside her, and to

Katrina's loving eye she looked the picture of woe.
A delightful picture, although she was crying—
something she was able to do without spoiling her
pretty face in the least. When she caught sight of
Katrina she cried: 'I haven't slept a wink all night,
I shall be ill . . .' She peered at her sister's
composed face. 'He's been here, hasn't he? I heard
him come in. I don't know how he dares after
what he's done!'

Katrina sat down on the edge of the bed. 'Well,
he didn't actually do anything, did he?'

Virginia looked at her in outraged astonishment.
'Not do anything? He doesn't want to marry me!'

'Yes, love, I know, and although it's a dreadful
thing to happen, it's better to say so now than wait
until you're married and regretting it.'

Virginia cast her a baleful look. 'What will
everyone say? And they'll all laugh—those hateful
Frobisher girls and Emily and Patricia and Sue . . .'

'Why should they laugh? They're your friends; it
could happen to them any time.'

'Oh, you're on his side—I might have known!'
Virginia sounded spiteful. 'Just because you're
getting on and not married yourself!'

Katrina went faintly pink. 'You don't mean a
word of that, love. But I do think it will be a great
pity if after all these years we shouldn't be on
speaking terms with Lucius—after all, he knew
you in your pram.'

Virginia tossed golden hair over one shoulder.
'What a silly girl you are, Katrina,' she observed,
and Katrina thought: twice in one morning,
Father used to say "Never mind the looks, the
girl's got a good head on her", but I haven't even
got that. She said placidly: 'Yes, I daresay I am.
Would you like to go away for a while, darling?'

Her sister's beautiful blue eyes opened wide. 'Go away? With the Hunt Ball only a few weeks off and James Lovell taking me up to town to see that new play everyone is talking about?' She smiled beguilingly. 'I do need a new dress, Katie.'

'You had that blue taffeta last month. What are you going to do about Lucius?'

'I won't speak to him again, and I hope you won't either.' She added viciously. 'I hope some perfectly frightful widow with a horde of children gets her hands on him—it's all he deserves!'

'I don't imagine he'll marry unless he wants to,' said Katrina, and instantly wished she hadn't as Virginia's tears began again. To stop them she promised a new dress, and the tears disappeared as if by magic.

She got up from the bed, observing mildly that James Lovell was on his way and shouldn't Virginia get dressed. At the door she paused to ask: 'Did Lucius actually ask you to marry him, love?'

Virginia was out of bed looking at herself in the dressing table mirror. 'Don't be such a nosey-parker,' she said crossly, 'I don't want to talk about it.' She smiled suddenly. 'Darling Katie, what would I do without you? You're the nicest person I know.'

Katrina spent the next hour going about her household duties. None of them were heavy, but all the same they had to be done; her parents had left them in comfortable circumstances—a charming Regency house with a splendid garden as well as the paddocks, Mrs Beecham, who had been with them since Katrina was born, Lovelace, who had been chauffeur, houseman and part-time gardener for almost the same length of time, and two girls from the village who came each day to help in the house. There was Old John too, who was what the villagers called a little light in the head; he came when it suited him and saw to the garden; he had a magic way with anything growing and no one had every thought of interfering with his work there.

She discussed food with Mrs Beecham, agreed that someone should come and re-hang the shutters outside the living room windows, suggested that Lovelace might like to take some harness to be repaired, whistled to Bouncer, the Black Labrador snoozing before the stove, and went into the garden to cut chrysanthemums. It was a clear day with frost underfoot and just for the moment warm enough for her to go outside in her tweed skirt and thick sweater, but with November half done, the days were getting short and she doubted if the weather would stay fine for much longer. She gathered her flowers and then walked on, round the house and up the sloping path which led to the kitchen gardens at the top of the slight hill. Old John was there, picking Brussels sprouts and talking to himself, and she joined him for a bit before crossing to the far wall where there was a stout wooden door.

She opened it but didn't go through, leaning against it and looking across the valley to where the chimneys of Stockley House sent pale wreaths of smoke into the clear air. The house was large, a great deal larger than her own home, with a park around it and a comfortable jumble of outbuildings, stables and barns at its back. Katrina knew every inch of it, for she had gone there very often as a child, first with her mother, when she went to call on Lucius's mother, and then on her own, to seek him out and plague him to let her go with him fishing or riding, but later on he went to school, and although she still went there frequently, she only saw him during the holidays, and when it was her turn to go to school she saw even less of him. All the same, they were firm friends and had remained so—until now. She hadn't always approved of his goings-on; by all accounts he was very much the man about town while he was in London—but that, she had told herself loyally, was his business, he was still Lucius; a friend to consult and someone to ask advice of, and when her parents were killed, a stout shoulder to cry into.

But as Virginia grew from a pretty little girl into a stunning young woman, he started to take her out; he took Katrina out too, riding or visiting friends, or walking the dogs, but when it came to dinner and the theatre in London, it was more often than not Virginia who was asked. And Katrina couldn't remember when her sister had persuaded him to take her to the Hunt Ball; she had done it so prettily that it would have been cruel to have refused her, and she herself, cheerfully protesting that she didn't care who she went with, had gone with the eldest Frobisher boy, a worthy young man, already going bald and forever nattering on about the obscure work he had to do at the Foreign Office. And after that, Lucius had taken Virginia each succeeding year—since she was seventeen. Not that he'd singled her out deliberately; he had a great many friends and went out with them all, never showing preference for any of the girls he knew, but gradually everyone came to take it for granted that he and Virginia intended to marry sooner or later, and indeed, Virginia made no effort to deny this, and Katrina, since the awful occasion when she had observed that it was nothing but gossip and been asked if she were jealous of her own sister, had kept silent.

As she watched a car came round the corner of the house and raced down the drive towards the big gates. That would be Lucius in his Jaguar, going up to London to do big business, she supposed. He'd be back by the evening, though, because Emily's mother was giving a dinner party and they had all been invited. Katrina made a mental resolve to warn Virginia to be polite at all costs.

As it happened there was no need; her sister told her over lunch that she was going out to dinner with James, and she didn't care who knew it.

'Then I'll phone Mrs Drake and say you've got a heavy cold,' said Katrina. 'That'll give her a chance to get someone else.'

Virginia gave her a pitying look. 'You always do the right thing, don't you? Say what you like—and I'm going up to town tomorrow to find a dress. What about you? I know you've no looks to speak of, but you've got a good figure—why don't you tart yourself up a bit?'

On the way up to the studio after lunch, Katrina stopped in front of the enormous wall mirror on the landing and took a good look at herself. Medium height, a little too plump, nice legs and hands and feet, a face unremarkable save for her eyes, pale brown hair expertly cut to frame it, and well cut, expensive clothes suitable to the life she led.

'Very dull,' she told her reflection, and went on up the small staircase to the next floor and into her studio, where she lost herself in the happy world of fairy tales. She was illustrating a new edition of Hans Andersen, and got carried away on a stream of elves and gnomes and princesses in distress. She painted until the light failed and went downstairs to the sitting room where they always had tea. There was no sign of Virginia, and Mrs Beecham, coming in with the tray, offered the information that Miss Virginia had gone out in the car not half an hour past.

'Well, we'll both be out this evening, Mrs Beecham, so don't wait up, will you? Whoever comes in last will lock up.'

Katrina poured herself a cup of tea, took a scone, picked up the daily paper and settled herself in a chair by the fire. The room was cosy, softly lighted and prettily furnished; her mother had always used it unless there had been people for tea—besides, there was no sense in having fires in the other, larger rooms unless there were guests. Bouncer was there too, and the two cats, lying in a friendly heap at her feet. She was a lucky young woman, she told herself soberly, to have so much when so many had so little. All the same, she felt a twinge of panic, glimpsing the years ahead. Supposing she didn't marry? And after all, she was turned twenty-seven and no one had actually asked her. Would she be content to stay here, painting and drawing and running the house and watching her friends grow old? And not being friends with Lucius any more?

She shook herself briskly. He had behaved very badly; come to think of it, he had changed over the recent years. His eyes could be as hard as stones on occasions, and he smiled a nasty little mocking smile far too often. The thought struck her that perhaps he was really in love with Virginia after all, but something had caused him to draw back from marrying her. He was a good deal older, of course, but that shouldn't matter; he was a handsome man and didn't look his age. There could be a girl somewhere, of course, but she discarded the thought at once. He wasn't devious, he would have made no bones about telling her that there was someone else. He had only laughed and said that poor Virginia had no heart. Katrina frowned; her sister was a darling—spoilt, perhaps, but who could help that, she was so enchantingly pretty and had such a way with her. To say that she was heartless was quite untrue.

Katrina bestirred herself, took Bouncer out for a run and went up to her room to change for the evening. She chose a dress with care. Lucius would be there and for some reason she wanted to look her very best—'Like a soldier cleaning his rifle before a battle,' she explained to Bouncer, who had made himself comfortable on the end of her bed.

The dress was soft green crêpe-de-chine, very simple, very expensive and just a shade too old for her. As most of her clothes were. Now that Virginia was grown up and went everywhere with her and to a great many parties on her own, Katrina had begun to think of herself as very much the older sister, and she dressed accordingly, which was a pity, for she had a pretty figure and a clear, unlined skin and looked a lot younger than her age. But even if she bought the wrong clothes, her taste in shoes was not to be faulted. They were her weakness; sensible enough during the day but replaced as soon as maybe by elegant high-heeled models by

Rayne and Gucci. She looked with satisfaction at the strappy kid slippers which went with the dress, slung on the quilted jacket she wore in the evenings if she was driving herself and went downstairs. There was no sign of Virginia and she wasn't in her room, so Katrina left a note for her and went outside to where Lovelace had parked the car for her, a Triumph Sports, quite elderly now but still going well. Lovelace had never quite approved of it, too fast for a young lady, he had averred, although he had to admit with the same breath that Miss Katrina was a first-class driver.

The Drakes lived five miles away in another village. As Katrina went down the drive and turned into the lane bordered by Stockley House's high wall, she thought with regret that normally Lucius would have called for her and driven her there and brought her home again. It was a sobering thought, rendered even more so when his Jaguar overtook her half way there, sliding sleekly past without him even turning his head, and even though it was dark, he would have known her car in the light of the headlamps. She watched his tail lights disappear round the next bend and felt lonely.

There were only a dozen people at the Drakes' house, and she knew them all, and since she was the last to arrive the drawing room was full enough for her to be able to avoid Lucius. Or so she thought.

She was sipping a dry sherry, which she detested, and listening to the Reverend Bartram Moffat's equally dry conversation, when he wandered over to them. He greeted them both affably, advised the Vicar that their host wanted advice about some parochial business and took up a position in front of her so that to escape would be difficult.

'Got over your nasty temper?' he wanted to know with what she considered to be sickening indulgence. She said: 'No,' and took another sip of sherry.

He took her glass from her, poured the contents into his own and gave her back the empty glass. 'You always hated the dry stuff,' he observed, 'and what you need at the moment is something sweet—I could pickle walnuts with your expression, Katie.'

She felt a bubble of laughter longing to escape, but all she said frostily was 'Indeed?'

'Where's our brokenhearted Virginia? I'm willing to bet Gem against Bouncer that she's gone out for the evening with young Lovell.'

Katrina twiddled her glass and went red. 'She needs comfort,' she observed.

'Rubbish, and you know it. Tell me, what are your plans? Am I to be ignored in future? Is the whole silly affair to be decently forgotten and a return made to the status quo, or do we speak to each other with icy civility in public and hate each other in private?'

She raised serious eyes to his. 'You know quite well that I could never hate you, Lucius, we've grown up together, we've been like brother and sister, but I don't want to be friends any more; maybe you weren't serious about Virginia, but you've hurt her deeply, and I can't forgive that.'

'All I hurt was her vanity and her pride.' He was staring down at her and the nasty little smile was there again. 'But have it your own way, my dear, although you're greatly mistaken.'

She didn't avoid his look. She said steadily: 'You have a lot of women friends—oh, I'm not curious, but people gossip, you know. That makes it so much worse, because Virginia is so young and you've known her since she was a baby.'

His voice was silky. 'And yet far better able to face the world and its wicked ways than you, Katie. We've had pleasant times together, haven't we? But in future I'll remember what you've said.' He smiled gently. 'I'm sure Mr Moffat is dying to talk to you again—such a nice quiet, well brought up young woman—and so correctly dressed.' The silky voice bit into her. 'You should change your style, Katrina, you're not thirty yet.' He moved aside to make room for Mr Moffat and she watched him go across the room to Mrs Drake. He looked handsome in his dinner jacket and his height and size made him noticeable wherever he was. She smiled politely at her companion and wondered miserably what it would be like to treat Lucius as a mere acquaintance when they met.

Dinner was a cheerful meal, since everyone there knew everyone else, and afterwards they sat around and talked for an hour or so until old Lady Ryder announced that she must go home, which was the signal for everyone else to do the same.

Katrina said her goodbyes, kissing the ladies and being kissed by the men, even Lucius, who brushed her cheek lightly and held her hand in an impersonal clasp and made some laughing remark about seeing her soon. And of course he'd been quite right to do it; in a day or two everyone would have heard that he and Virginia had broken up, but until then no one needed to know. She had felt mean listening to kind Mrs Drake's concern for Virginia's cold, and then seethed as she caught Lucius's cynical look as he overheard. The comfortable, dependable man she had known all her life had changed into a remote, mocking stranger with cold eyes.

Driving back, she debated as to whether he was hiding a broken heart under that deadpan face, and if so what she could do about it.

Nothing; one didn't interfere with other people's lives even with the best of intentions, although she could wheedle Virginia into telling her what had happened. She would have to wait for the right moment, of course.

Which came a good deal sooner than she had expected. She was in the house, sitting at the kitchen table drinking the hot chocolate Mrs Beecham had left out, when she heard the front door open and close, and a moment later her sister came into the kitchen.

'Hullo,' said Katrina. 'Did you lock up?'

Virginia gave her a dreamy look. 'No, was I supposed to?'

Katrina got up. 'Never mind, I'll do it. There's loads of chocolate if you'd like a cup.'

'After two bottles of champagne? You must be joking! Did you have a very dull evening?'

'I'd enjoyed it.' Katrina spoke over her shoulder on the way to the hall and the front door. When she got back, Virginia was curled up in Mrs Beecham's chair by the Aga.

'Was Lucius there?' she asked.

'Yes, of course.'

'Did you talk to him?'

'Yes—not much, though.'

'No one knew? That he'd jilted me?'

'No, Virginia—did he jilt you? Had he asked

you to marry him? And had you said yes?'

Virginia closed her eyes and yawned. 'What a lot of questions! Aren't you being a bit nosey, darling?' She went on softly: 'He's made a fool of me, and he's going to pay for it.'

Katrina took her cup to the sink. 'How can you talk like that when you expected to marry him? You must have loved—still love—him.'

Her sister got up and strolled to the door. 'Darling, you're the wee-est bit behind the times— in fact, it's the sort of thing Mummy might have said; or even Nanny. I can see I must update you.' She smiled seraphically. 'I shall have to think of something.' She blew a kiss. 'Goodnight, Katie.'

Katrina went to bed presently, but not to sleep. Virginia had made a remarkably quick recovery from her broken heart; on the other hand, she was probably hiding her real feelings under a cheerful exterior. It was natural enough that she should be angry with Lucius, especially as he was so annoyingly cheerful about the whole thing. It was to be hoped that when their feelings had cooled, they could settle down again. Virginia was very young; she was bound to fall in love again. Katrina fell into an uneasy sleep and woke late, the remnants of a dream provokingly not to be recalled filling her head. It had been as nasty a dream as possible, of that she was sure.

It was strange not seeing Lucius. He had been in the habit of strolling in at least once each day, to offer lifts, or go riding, or just to sit for half an hour and talk. He was a good landlord and the estate, although not large, took up a good deal of his day, and twice a week he drove up to London where he was a partner in a large accounting firm. Katrina had got into the habit of giving him little commissions—something special from Fortum and Mason, an order for the wine merchants, a query on a Harrods account, and besides that, getting a lift whenever she wanted one. She busied herself with her painting, glad she had a deadline to meet and no time for idling. She would take her work up to the publishers at the end of the week and see if she could find a dress for the Hunt Ball.

Virginia had gone up to London and come back with a ravishing ball gown which had cost a staggering sum of money, and now that important matter had been settled, she spent a good deal of her time with her various friends. Katrina had been surprised that no one had said anything about her sister and Lucius, but then she hadn't been out very much, giving the excuse that she had to finish her work and was pushed d for time. Now she was just about finished, and since Virginia had phoned to say that she was going to stay a night or two with Emily and Patricia, it left her free to do as she wanted. It would do poor little Virginia good to stay with her friends; she had gone over for lunch, and as she had often stopped the night, Katrina had welcomed it. Besides, the roads could be treacherous now that the weather was turning really wintry. The Turners didn't live all that far away, a matter of ten miles or so, but Virginia was a careless drive..

Katrina tidied away her paints and brushes and began to wrap up her work. It was still early, so she could drive up to London and hand over her work, have lunch and look for a dress—but that would mean driving back in the evening, not that that worried her, she was a good driver, but suppose Virginia decided to return home earlier? Besides, it left her short of time.

She was tying the tapes of the portfolio when the door opened and Lucius walked in. She was so surprised to see him that she didn't say anything at all, only stood staring at him. He crossed the big room towards her, his movements as leisurely as usual, but she detected a fine rage under his bland expression. She said good morning in a questioning voice and resisted the urge to back away from him.

'Is it? Where is Virginia, Katrina?' he asked as he came to a halt in front of her.

'Spending a couple of days with the Turners. Why?'

'Very wise of her.' His voice was even, but his eyes were grey stones. 'Do you know what she's told all our friends and acquaintances? No, I can see you don't. That I've cast her off—her own words—and taken up with you!'

'Me?' asked Katrina, quite flabbergasted.

'Oh, yes. You see, as she has explained at some length to everyone who would listen, she had no chance against your brains and elegance and— er—knowledge of the world—oh, and I almost forgot—your maturity.'

Katrina goggled at him. 'But what nonsense!' she managed.

'Oh, no, just a clever way of putting things, my dear. When everyone has got over their open-mouthed astonishment and thought about it, they'll see it for the nonsense it is. In the meantime . . .' he managed to smile thinly, 'I should like to wring her neck!'

'She's upset,' said Katrina. 'She said her heart was broken . . .'

'And what else, I wonder? That I was an ogre,

that I should pay for upsetting her careful plans—
you know what she intended to do?'

'No, but she—she did say you would pay for it.
I don't think for one minute that she meant it.'

He said quite savagely: 'You walk around with
your head in the clouds, painting hobgoblins and
flower fairies, you let Virginia trample you
underfoot and wheedle you into giving her far too
much money. Why in heaven's name don't you use
some of it on yourself? Buy some clothes suited to
your age!' He saw her colour painfully. 'Oh, you
always look nice, but why think of yourself as a
woman, a staid woman at that, who'll never see
forty again? You're twenty-seven and you look ten
years younger than that.' He laughed softly. 'And
I'm not paying compliments—I know you too well
for that.'

'What are you going to do?' asked Katrina, not
liking the sound of that laugh.

'Do? Why, call her bluff, of course. I shall turn
my attentions to you, Katie. In due course we shall
become engaged, and when you've had the time to
gather together whatever it is girls gather before
they marry, we'll be wed. Here in Upper Tew.'

For a big man he was very fast on his feet.
Before she could gather her wits to answer such
nonsense, he had left her, closing the door very
quietly behind him.

CHAPTER TWO

ALL idea of going to London gone from her head, Katrina sat down and allowed her chaotic thoughts to settle themselves. They jostled each other around her head, making no sense. Lucius had been joking—or had he? And surely Virginia would not have played such a rotten trick even if she had meant it as a joke. She must have known it was a bad one, sure to misfire. Katrina thanked heaven that their friends, mostly lifelong, would think twice before believing Virginia, or at least they wouldn't accuse her of lying, merely of exaggerating, and that because her youthful ego had been deflated. And no one, no one at all, would have anything to say against Lucius. She sighed; which meant that Virginia would have to explain. She frowned then. Surely her sister hadn't said those hurtful things?—as though she had ever made any push to attract Lucius away from Virginia, and she wasn't brainy or mature or elegant, that had been cruel. All the same, Lucius need not have been quite so angry, and the suggestion he had made had been ridiculous. If he thought he was going to get even with Virginia by playing a silly makebelieve game with herself as an unwilling partner he could think again! She finished tying the portfolio and went downstairs.

In the sitting room Lucius was sitting comfortably, reading *The Times*. He got up as she stopped just inside the door, taking no notice of her astonished: 'Well, what are you doing here?'

'I heard you telling Mrs Drake that you intended going up to town with your drawings. I'll drive you up now; I've an appointment for later on this morning, but I'll pick you up and bring you back any time you like.'

Katrina said with great dignity: 'Thank you, Lucius, but I shall drive myself up tomorrow. I'm surprised at you asking.'

'My dear, didn't I make myself plain? For lack of a better phrase, I intend to court you. I shouldn't like to make Virginia out to be a liar.'

'And what about me?' asked Katrina furiously. 'No one's asked me if—if I want to be courted.' She added snappishly: 'How silly and old-fashioned that sounds!'

'Ah, yes indeed; you must add these to my other shortcomings.'

'Don't be ridiculous! You're being tiresome.'

'That too,' he agreed gravely. 'How long will it take you to get ready?'

'I've just said, I'm going to drive myself . . .' She caught his eye, grey and cold and compelling. 'Very well,' she said reluctantly, 'but I don't want any more of this roses nonsense. I shall talk to Virginia when she gets back and—and . . .' She faltered under his amused stare.

'You haven't a chance,' he told her. 'She's always made rings round you and always will.' He nodded gently at her. 'Go and get ready.'

Ever since she could remember Katrina had obeyed him unquestioningly, even though at times she hadn't minced matters if she was annoyed with him. She went back upstairs to her room and changed into a dark grey suit, beautifully cut. It was elegant and in excellent taste, and made her look older than she was. A scarf, plain court shoes and a matching handbag completed her outfit while doing nothing for her at all. She fetched her portfolio and went downstairs to tell Mrs Beecham that she wouldn't be back until the late afternoon, before going back to the sitting room.

Lucius eyed her thoughtfully. 'Going to do any shopping?' he wanted to know.

'Well, I thought I might look round for a dress for the Hunt Ball. Why do you want to know?'

He shrugged his shoulders. 'No reason. Shall we go?'

He dropped her off at the publishers in Bloomsbury after arrranging to meet her for lunch at the Connaught Hotel. I'll be in the bar at twelve-thirty and wait for you,' he suggested.

She stood on the pavement outside the publishers' office. 'But will you be ready by then? I could make it later if you like and do some shopping first.'

He handed her the portfolio. 'No need, I'll be there. You can shop after lunch.'

He waited until she had gone inside and then got back into the car and drove off. Katrina watched him go through the glass doors. It was strange to think that despite all the happenings of the last few days, she felt exactly the same about him as she had always done—a friend, someone to be depended upon, who always knew what to do. As she gave her name to the receptionist she decided that the best plan would be to ignore their extraordinary conversation of that morning; she would have it out with Virginia, persuade her to tell everyone that she had been joking, and everything would be just as it had been. Or would it be? She had no chance to ponder the matter before she was ushered upstairs to the publishers' office.

She wasn't there long. The illustrations were approved, she was asked if she would undertake another commission for a jacket cover, given coffee, promised a cheque within a few days, and took her departure. She had to walk a little way before she could get a taxi and the traffic was heavy. She got to the Connaught ten minutes late, to find Lucius sitting in the bar with no sign of impatience.

She sat down opposite him and took off her gloves. 'Sorry,' she said, 'I couldn't find a taxi. Have you been waiting long?'

'A few minutes. What will you drink?'

Over their drinks they talked without saying much. Katrina felt awkward; it hadn't been so bad in the car, sitting beside him while they carried on desultory conversation, but now with him opposite her, his grey eyes friendly, she had the absurd wish to ask his advice about what she should do. However, she didn't. She told him about her new commission, enlarging upon the weather, which was chilly, and agreed nervously when he suggested that they might lunch without further delay.

She discovered that she was hungry once they were seated, to Lucius's suggestion that they might try the smoked trout she agreed immediately, and then went on to boeuf Stroganoff and ruche glacée. It was over their coffee that Lucius suggested that as he was free for the afternoon he might accompany her on her shopping expedition.

'You'd be bored stiff,' said Katrina forthrightly.

'No, I won't. We'll leave the car here and walk.'

'But I thought of going to Harrods or Liberty's.'

'Let's try Bond Street and Sloane Street first.'

They were on the steps of the hotel when she said: 'Look, you'll hate it—tagging from shop to shop, and I never go to boutiques . . .'

He took her arm and began walking her along the pavement. 'Why not?'

'I'm not that sort of girl—I mean, I'm not smart or pretty.' She added pettishly: 'And for heaven's sake, why do you ask? You've known it for years.'

'I know a couple of shops where I'm sure you'll see you're mistaken.'

She stopped walking to look up at him. She didn't mind in the least that he hadn't denied her lack of good looks; during all their years of friendship he had never made any bones about that, but she was curious about something else. 'How do you know about boutiques?' she wanted to know.

Lucius chuckled. 'Don't be so inquisitive, Katie.' He walked her on again and presently stopped before an elegant plate glass window, sheltering a vase of flowers, a gossamer scarf over a little gilt chair, and a black dress, displayed on an impossibly slim plaster model.

'That's a nice little chair,' observed Katrina, who was interested in furniture.

'Charming, but you can't wear that to the Hunt Ball,' he said as he opened the door and swept her inside.

Dove grey velvet, more little chairs, delicate lights and an elegant creature in black crêpe left Katrina without words. But it was obvious that Lucius had no intention of helping her. She asked to see some evening dresses and shot him a smouldering look.

The saleslady smiled with quite a human

warmth. 'For yourself, of course, madam. Had you any particular colour in mind?'

Lucius had made himself comfortable on a buttonbacked sofa in one corner. 'Green,' he suggested. 'That bright peacock green-blue—taffeta, if you've got such a thing.'

Katrina went and sat beside him on the sofa. 'I never wear bright colours,' she hissed.

'That's the trouble, my dear.' He turned to look at the saleslady, followed by another one, bearing an armful of all the colours of the rainbow. 'Try them all on.'

'Size twelve?' fluted the saleslady. 'Madam has a slim figure, and of course we can do any alterations necessary.' She signed to the other girl, who held a patterned organza creation in shades of green. It had a full skirt and a frill around its low neckline. 'Or this,' she coaxed, and displayed a rose taffeta with long tight sleeves and a square neck. 'Or perhaps this is the colour?'

She was a good saleswoman; she had merely whetted Katrina's appetite with the first two; the third was exactly what Lucius had suggested—taffeta in a rich green shot through with blue with short billowing sleeves, a tiny bodice and wide skirts. 'Try them all on, madam,' she begged again.

Katrina didn't look at Lucius. He really had a nerve, bulldozing her into coming into a shop like this in the first place, sitting there like a possessive husband! She wasn't going to buy anything, just to teach him a lesson, but since she was there, she might just try them on . . .

The organza was charming, not at all her usual sort of dress, and it certainly did something for her. Without asking the saleslady swept back the

silk curtains and invited her to show herself to Sir,
and since there was not any way out of that, she
did so, rather shyly.

'Very nice.' He studied her for such a long time
that she frowned a little and went back into the
dressing room, where she tried the pink, which was
even prettier.

'I like that,' declared Lucius, 'but let's see that
green thing first.'

The green thing was exactly right, although so
different to her other evening gowns that she
hardly recognised herself. Lucius took his time
looking her over. 'That's the one,' he said finally.
'I like the neck.'

Katrina pinkened. The neck was low, not at all
the kind of thing she usually wore—now Virginia
would look gorgeous in it . . .

'Madam has splendid shoulders and a very
pretty bustline,' observed the saleslady. 'If I might
say so, the dress is just right for her.'

Katrina kept her eyes on the silk wallpaper
above Lucius's head. 'I'm not sure . . .' she began.

'Have it, Katie, and the pink one as well.'

She was quite out of her depth. Years of going
to one of the better stores and choosing the
unobtrusive clothes which she had always believed
helped her to be a little less plain hadn't prepared
her for this. Now she was landed with two eye-
catching dresses she might never wear. She
changed back into her well cut suit, tidied her hair,
and, once more the self-possessed young woman,
went back into the shop to find the dresses already
packed and Lucius putting away his cheque book.
It was hardly the place to argue. She waited until
they were out of the shop before she started.

'There was no need for you to pay. I've plenty

of money of my own. Whatever did the woman think?'

He took her reluctant arm. 'I've never minded what people think. In any case, why are you fussing about it? You can give me a cheque later.'

'I've no idea how much they were—and what on earth shall I do with two dresses? I'm not even sure that I'll wear one of them.'

'You'll wear the green thing to the Hunt Ball, and the pink will come in handy when we go dancing.' He glanced down at her. 'Have you forgotten that we're walking out?'

'We're not—I won't . . . I shall speak to Virginia when she gets home!'

'So you said.' Lucius had stopped before another shop window. 'Now, that's nice,' he pointed out the brown velvet suit draped over a stand, its matching blouse in a deep cream silk cast negligently by it.

Katrina took a look. 'Chanel,' she observed. 'It'll be hundreds of pounds.'

'You said only a few minutes ago that you had plenty of money.' He added smoothly: 'Dressed in that you'd easily get the better of Virginia. Buy it.'

Katrina, who had had no intention of buying anything else, found herself in the shop, trying on the suit which was a perfect fit, and since she might as well be hanged for a sheep as for a lamb, trying the blouse as well, writing a cheque for a heart-stopping sum, and walking out of the shop again. Outside she said firmly: 'I'm not buying another thing—I could have got two good tweed outfits for that money . . .'

'So you could, but think how nice you look in that coat and skirt. Worth every penny. I like the little jacket; as that other woman said, you have a very pretty bosom, you should show it off more.'

Katrina gasped. 'Well, really, Lucius, whatever will you say next.'

'Well, surely we've known each other long enough for me to make a few brotherly remarks without you coming over all modest?' A gleam came into his eye. 'Why, I remember—let me see, I must have been about twelve and you five—we went swimming in the river, and you without a stitch on.'

Katrina let out a gurgle of laughter. 'Oh, I remember—Nanny gave me such a ticking off and a good smacking.'

'And I had a painful interview with Father in the study.'

'We deserved it, I suppose—it was March, wasn't it? We could have died of cold.'

They had tea in a small tea-room, waited upon by a refined young lady in a chintz overall; China tea and mammoth eclairs. Katrina, about to start on her second cake, arrested her fork in mid-air when Lucius said:

'You'll get fat, Katie.'

She looked at him in horror. 'No—am I fat now? Even a little plump?'

'Just right—don't for God's sake go on a diet, though—skinny women have no charm.'

Katrina took a good bite. 'Oh, good—all the same, I must remember to weigh myself sometimes.' She smiled at him across the little table. 'What a strange day it's been; like a dream.'

'Every second of it true, Katrina. Who is taking you to the Hunt Ball?'

'Well, several men have offered . . .'

'But you've not accepted?'

'No.'

'Then you'll come with me. You were coming to the dinner party first anyway, weren't you?'

'Yes, but what about Virginia? I mean, won't you feel—well, awkward?'

He gave her a cool stare. 'Why should I? There'll be a dozen of us there anyway, and she and I are bound to meet again, you know.'

'Yes, but after the things she said . . .'

'Silly, childish nonsense. Shall I send the car for you or will you drive over?'

'I'll drive.'

He nodded. You can leave the car at my place and pick it up later.'

They walked back presently and got into the car and began the drive home. 'Doing anything this evening?' asked Lucius idly.

'No—I don't expect Virginia until tomorrow. I'll sketch some ideas for the book jacket.'

'We can call in at your place and you can make sure she hasn't come home and then have dinner with me.' He added wickedly: 'We have to get to know each other, you know.'

'What rubbish—we've known each other all our lives. Besides, I'd rather like a quiet evening.'

'When have you ever found me noisy?' he wanted to know, 'and I promise I'll drive you home the moment you want to go.'

There was no message from Virginia when they reached her home. Mrs Beecham received Katrina's news that she would be dining with Lucius with a straight face but a decided twinkle in her shrewd eyes. All she said was: 'I know where you are if you're wanted, Miss Katrina. Will you be late back? Lovelace can take Bouncer for his walk.'

'I'll not be late, Mrs Beecham. Will you get someone to take these boxes up to my room?' She bent to scratch Bouncer's head and Lucius, standing by the door, said: 'Bring him with you, you know how he likes a romp with my two.'

So Bouncer scrambled into the back of the car and stuck his head between them as they drove back into the lane and, after a moment or so, turned in at the gates of Stockley House. Katrina was as familiar with the house as her own home, but it never ceased to give her a thrill as she got out before its massive entrance. The front of the house was Queen Anne; only at the back were there the remains of the Tudor house which had been the first Massey home. The porch was a magnificent one, leading to a vast door opening on to a small vestibule which in turn gave on to the front hall, a circular apartment with a great many doors and a double staircase taking up the whole of the far wall. The ceiling was painted and gilded and the white panelled walls were hung with paintings. Katrina said a cheerful 'Good evening' to Cobb, the middle-aged and spidery man who had opened the door, and walked past him, Bouncer beside her. But not for long; one of the doors was open and two dogs came bounding out, a Great Dane puppy and a Dalmatian. They fell upon their master with every sign of delight and then joined Bouncer. Lucius walked past her, through the open door, and opened the doors leading on to the terrace beyond the room, and the three of them streamed out, barking with pleasure.

'They can let off steam for a bit,' he commented, coming back into the hall. 'You'd like a drink? Want to do your face? You know which room, I'll be in the drawing room.'

Katrina nodded and crossed the hall to the staircase. On the way she paused to look at one of the portraits. 'I see Buxom Bessy's still here—she ought to be hidden away in a guestroom.'

Lucius had strolled across to join her and they stood looking up at the painting of an extremely plump lady in a remarkably low-cut gown and a fearsome wig. 'She has a certain air . . .' he began, and Katrina giggled.

'The Lucius Massey who married her thought she was enchanting; she was probably very pretty when he first met her. He must have continued to think so, because he loved her until she died.'

'Poor Bessy—ten children too!'

'Not as bad as it sounds, though. There would have been nursemaids enough, and tutors and governesses.'

Katrina started up the stairs. 'Well, I suppose with all those children one would need plenty of help. Ten is an awful lot.'

'Too many? You dislike large families? I know they're not fashionable.'

Katrina turned round to face him. 'Not so much unfashionable as anti-social! But of course I'd like two or three of my own, and in a house like this, or ours, for that matter, there's room enough. Besides, there's money enough too—I've even got an old nanny pretending she's retired—so have you, Lucius.'

'We can count ourselves among the lucky ones, then, can't we?'

Something in his voice made her turn back and run up the staircase. As she walked along the gallery above the hall she had a vague fleeting picture of children running round the big house, sliding down the banisters, shouting and laughing. One day, she supposed, Lucius would marry—she had begun to think of him as married to Virginia, but that had come to an end; he'd fall in love again. Had he ever been in love with Virginia? She opened a door at the end of the gallery and entered a small, very pretty bedroom and sat down before a white-painted dressing table to do her face and hair. Once or twice she had slept in this room; when she had been a little girl and gone to stay with the Masseys on some special occasion, and ever since, even after Lucius's parents died, it had been known as her room. She went downstairs presently and found Lucius before a great log fire in the drawing room. He got up as she went in, sat her down in a small armchair opposite his and gave her a drink.

It was a very pleasant room and comfortable despite its size and grandeur, and presently he got up and let the three dogs in. They jostled for places before the fire, sinking into a contented heap, piled on top of each other, the puppy with his head on Lucius's shoes.

Katrina, curled up in her chair, gave a small sigh of contentment. There was no need to make conversation, she and Lucius knew each other too well for that. She was half asleep when Cobb came to say that dinner was served, and although she was wide awake once they were at table, their talk was of mundane things—the new village hall, plans for the Christmas party at the church school, who could be roped in for the carol singing, could old Mrs Todd, who'd lived in a tiny cottage in the village for untold years, be left to live alone much longer or should something be done about getting her some help—tactfully, of course, she was an old woman with a sharp tongue and a mind of her own even at ninety odd years.

They went back to the drawing room for their

coffee and presently Katrina said reluctantly: 'I must go—it's getting late, and Lovelace will stay up for me even though I've a key.'

Lucius made no effort to stop her. She put on her jacket and got into the car beside him and he drove her the short distance back home. He got out when she did and she asked: 'Do you want to come in?' with a lack of enthusiasm which made him chuckle. 'No,' he told her, 'only to see you safely indoors.'

He waited after he had opened the door for her until Lovelace came into the hall and until he heard Katrina ask if Virginia was back. Only when Lovelace shook his head did he say goodnight, adding as he went through the door: 'Remember to wear the new outfit tomorrow, Katie.'

She hadn't thought anything about that until just before tea on the next day; there had been several things to do, indoors and out, and she felt untidy. Once in her room, showered and peering into her cupboard for something to wear, she saw the brown velvet hanging. Lucius had suggested that she should put it on—a silly idea, since she wasn't expecting anyone. Virginia hadn't phoned; she would be staying another night, probably. All the same, it would give her rather dull day a bit of life.

She put it on and studied herself in the pier glass. There was no denying the fact that it did something for her; the blouse was exactly right and the straight little jacket with its braid trimming was elegant, as was the pencil-slim skirt. She put on a pair of brown shoes she hardly ever wore because she had decided that they were too frivolous. Now they looked exactly right too. She went downstairs feeling rather pleased with herself, had her tea before the fire in the sitting room and sat down at her desk to do her accounts. She had spent far too much money yesterday and she still owed Lucius for the two dresses, and heaven knew how much they would be. There was her cheque to come, of course, and the new commission, and the dividends from various shares. All the same, she would have to be careful; the lodge roof needed repairs, and there was a broken fence to be mended. The winter months were always expensive too with the house to keep warm, and people in for drinks around Christmas. Katrina chewed the top of her pen and did her careful sums, and didn't hear the car coming up the drive.

The sudden brilliance of light as the wall lights were switched on from the door made her turn round. Virginia was home.

Katrina got up unhurriedly. 'Hullo,' she said. 'I wasn't sure when you'd be back.'

Her sister was staring at her and didn't answer, but after a moment she said: 'That's new, and it must have cost a bomb—you look positively elegant!'

Lucius had been quite right. The suit had wrapped Katrina in a pleasant aura of knowing that she looked her best, and consequently sure of herself. She said lightly: 'I thought it was high time that I lived up to the image you've given me.'

Virginia looked guilty and at the same time defiant. 'Well, I didn't see why everyone should go around saying Poor Virginia.' She added sharply: 'I said I'd get even with Lucius.'

'So you did,' agreed Katrina calmly, 'but did you have to get even with me too?—I can't remember trespassing on your preserves.'

Virginia tossed her head. 'You're not exactly

what I'd call a serious rival. Were you thinking of having a go?'

'At what?'

'Why, Lucius, of course. After all, he'll have to marry some time, though I should think you'd be bored stiff with each other—after all you've known each other for years and years.'

'I can't say the idea had crossed my mind,' said Katrina in a cold little voice, 'and I'm sure Lucius . . .'

She stopped herself just in time; it had crossed his mind, hadn't it? but only because it suited his own ends.

'What's all this about me?' Lucius's voice was casually placid. Katrina wondered how long he'd been standing by the open door listening to them. He strolled into the room and went to stand by the fire.

'So you're back, you silly girl,' he observed to Virginia. 'You've made a fine fool of yourself, haven't you? I hope it teaches you a lesson—that not every man who dates you wants to be saddled with you for the rest of his life.'

Virginia's pretty face flushed scarlet. 'You beast! Katrina, listen to him—say something!'

'Don't hide behind your sister,' advised Lucius pleasantly. 'You're quite able to stand up for yourself.' He glanced at his watch. 'Katrina, if we're going out to dinner we must go now—I've booked the table for half past seven.'

Katrina stared at him. He was smiling a little, but the look he gave her was sufficient for her to say hastily: 'I'm ready—I must just get my bag, and I suppose I'd better bring a coat.'

She saw Virginia's puzzled look as she went past her and up to her room. It was a pity that Lucius had come when he had, because they had merely postponed the unpleasant half hour she and Virginia were going to have. And where in heaven's name were they going? She flung a few things into a clutch bag, got a coat from the cupboard and went downstairs again.

Lucius was standing exactly where she had left him, Virginia sitting on the arm of a chair. Katrina heard her voice very clearly as she went across the hall. 'And don't think I'm coming to your stuffy dinner party for the Hunt Ball! James is taking me out first, and we'll come on to the ball later.'

'Afraid to face them?' asked Lucius softly, and went to meet Katrina, who paused in the doorway to say: 'I told Mrs Beecham dinner at half past seven, I shan't be late back.'

She didn't wait to hear Virginia's muttered reply, but went out to where the Jaguar was parked and got in beside Lucius. As he drove off she said: 'Now you can explain, Lucius.'

'I thought we might have a meal at La Sorbonne—we haven't been there for quite a time. Virginia didn't care for Oxford, we nearly always went up to town or to Bath.'

Katrina said, 'Oh,' and searched for a suitable reply, but she couldn't think of one, so instead she said: 'Why?'

They were on the main road, the Jaguar making light of the twenty odd miles they had to drive. 'I thought it might be nice to give that new suit an airing.'

'You didn't know that Virginia was coming home this evening?' she persisted.

'My dear girl, how suspicious you are! How should I know that, and how could I have booked a table on the spur of the moment without you knowing?'

Which made sense. She wasn't going to know that he had seen the lights of Virginia's car going up the lane, shouted to Cobb to phone La Sorbonne and followed her as quickly as he could. Virginia had a nasty temper and Katrina was no match for her, even in the new outfit.

They didn't talk much, but since over the years they had attained an easy relationship which didn't need constant conversation to keep it alive, Katrina accepted Lucius's silence and sat quietly, lulled into a peaceful state where she didn't even bother to think. They reached Oxford presently and Lucius turned off the High Street, parked the car and walked her down the little alley close by. The restaurant was on the first floor of a seventeenth-century house and was noted for its excellent food. Katrina wrinkled her small nose at the scent of the flowers on the table and said: 'This is nice!'

Lucius smiled at her. 'Good. That brown thing is very becoming, Katie.' His glance was as careless as a brother's. 'What would you like to drink?'

They dined at leisure; wild duck, cooked as only it could be cooked at La Sorbonne, preceded by globe artichokes and followed by a lemon sorbet. They sat over their coffee, talking like the old friends they were, but not mentioning Virginia. It wasn't until they were back again and Katrina was saying goodbye that Lucius asked: 'Aren't you going to ask me in for a drink?'

Katrina said forthrightly: 'Heavens, whatever for? Though if you really want one, I could make coffee or tea . . .'

'Tea would be nice,' said Lucius so meekly that she looked at him suspiciously, but since she couldn't see him very clearly she said reluctantly: 'All right, come in then.'

Lucius smiled a little and followed her into the quiet house, across the hall and through the baize door to the kitchen. It was comfortably warm, the Aga glowing gently and Cromwell, Mrs Beecham's cat, curled up before it. Lucius filled a kettle and set it to boil while Katrina fetched two mugs and found the milk and sugar, then sat down at the big scrubbed table. The tea was strong and hot. 'We shan't sleep a wink,' declared Katrina, and poured second cups.

They had almost finished when the door opened and Virginia came in, a vision in pink velvet and chiffon frills. 'I heard the car,' she observed, 'and the racket Lucius made crossing the hall. I think it's very selfish of you to make so much noise—I need my sleep.'

Katrina was on the point of saying she was sorry, but Lucius forestalled her. 'Did you come all the way down here to tell us that?' he asked. 'I very much doubt it.'

Virginia shot him a cross look. 'How did you guess? As a matter of fact, I forgot to tell you something when I came home this evening.'

'Let me guess,' said Lucius smoothly. 'You're engaged—James Lovell, of course, I can't think of anyone else who would have you.'

'You knew—how did you find out?' Virginia was so furiously angry that she began to cry, and Katrina started forward to comfort her, to be firmly checked by Lucius.

'I didn't know, but there is such a thing as logical reasoning. Are you going to wait for a decent interval before you announce it? I mean, it's only days since I—er—threw you over, and you must give people time to recover from that, you know.'

'If James were here, he'd knock you down,' sobbed Virginia.

'I very much doubt that, but he's welcome to try next time we meet. Now go to bed, you silly girl.'

'Virginia . . .' began Katrina.

'Oh, shut up!' Her eyes narrowed. 'It'll serve you right if you stay a starchy spinster for the rest of your days!' She rounded on Lucius. 'And as for you . . .'

'Burning oil or slow poison—goodnight, Virginia, and congratulations.'

When she had gone Katrina said slowly: 'You needn't have been so unkind.' She added: 'All the same, I'm glad you were here.'

Lucius collected the mugs and put them tidily in the sink. All he said was: 'May I come to lunch tomorrow?' And when she said 'Yes' in a surprised voice: 'I fancy Virginia will have more to say by then, and Katie, don't, I beg of you, get embroiled in an argument with her until I get here.'

'That's all very well! She's my sister, I've always taken care of her . . .'

'Just so. I wonder when you'll realise that you're the one who needs taking care of?'

He crossed the space between them and threw an arm round her shoulders. 'Don't worry about it, and there's one thing I can promise you; you're not a starchy spinster and never will be.' He dropped a kiss on the top of her head. 'Go to bed.'

'You were joking, weren't you?' she asked in a small voice.

He understood her at once. 'No. We'll announce our engagement at the Hunt Ball . . . no, better still, at Virginia's wedding. If I know her, she'll

make James get a special licence and expect a slap-
up wedding in about ten days' time.'

He took her arm and went into the hall. 'Lock
up after me,' he warned her, and went out of the
door to the car.

Katrina shut the bolts and turned the key, her
head a muddle of weddings, engagements and
Lucius's arrogance in taking it for granted that she
wanted to marry him. She tumbled into bed
presently, all these problems swept away by the
enormous one of how to arrange a big wedding in
a matter of days. Ten days, Lucius had said, and
from experience she knew that he was almost
always right.

CHAPTER THREE

When Katrina went down to breakfast the next morning, Lovelace met her in the hall with the information that Miss Virginia was having her breakfast in bed as she had had a bad night so Katrina shared hers with the ever faithful Bouncer, then went back upstairs and tapped on her sister's door.

Virginia was sitting up in bed, her breakfast tray beside her, reading a magazine. She looked up as Katrina went in, then bent her head over its glossy pages again.

Katrina took the magazine from her and sat down on the edge of the bed. She asked: 'When were you planning to get married, Virginia?'

'Soon—before Christmas, though I can't see what business it is of yours.' She snatched the magazine back, looking sulky.

'Well, I supposed you'd want a pretty wedding, and that will take some organising. Invitations and bridesmaids and so on . . .'

'Don't you mind if I get married and you don't?'

'Well, no, I don't think so—why should I? I don't want to marry James.' Katrina paused. 'You're sure, Virginia?—it's only a few days ago since you thought you wanted to marry Lucius.'

She didn't give her sister time to answer. Virginia's hands had curled round the magazine, her eyes blazing, and Katrina remembered that Lucius had told her to wait until he was there, and she suddenly wished he was. She got up and went out of the room, and the magazine thudded on the door as she was closing it behind her.

She'd been a fool to try and talk to Virginia. She was shaking a little as she went downstairs and set about her normal chores, first to Mrs Beecham to let her know that Lucius would be there for lunch, then out into the garden with Bouncer to find old John and coax him to let her have some of the Doyenne du Comice pears he had been picking with such care. They were a crop that he tended with pleasure and pride and each autumn he tended to hand them out in a miserly fashion. But this morning he was in a generous mood, and when Katrina explained that Mr Massey was coming to lunch and might enjoy one, he presented her with a small basket of the fruit.

'That old Pritchard down at Stockley House, 'e don't know a good pear when he sees 'un, though 'e's got a good eye for a grape.'

Katrina perched on a pile of wooden boxes, took an apple from one of the trays and prepared for half an hour's conversation with the old man. It was only the appearance of the gardener's boy with a jug of tea for old John that sent her on her way, this time to the stables.

There were only two horses there now, her own little mare and a large bony creature, very good-natured, used for carting and odd jobs around the grounds. There was a donkey too, very old now, living in happy retirement except for once a year, when at the summer Church Fête he gave rides to the small children. Katrina pottered happily, getting in the way of Lovelace who was polishing the harness and keeping an eye on the young boy who came up from the village to clean out the stables. It was only as the stable clock struck noon that she went back to the house to put on a blouse instead of the sweater she was wearing and do things to her hair and face.

She went downstairs presently and found Lucius sitting comfortably before the fire in the sitting room, reading a newspaper, and since he had been in and out of the house ever since she could remember, she said without surprise: 'Hullo—did you give yourself a drink?'

He got to his feet. 'No, I waited for you. Is Virginia joining us?'

'I expect so—she didn't say she wasn't.' She accepted a glass of sherry and sat down.

'You've already seen her?' She thought he sounded mildly curious.

'Well, yes, just to say good morning. She didn't come down to breakfast—she had a bad night.'

He said: 'Naturally,' in a voice so dry that she was on the point of asking him what he meant when Virginia came in.

'You!' she exclaimed with loathing, and stopped just inside the door.

'Don't be childish,' he begged her 'and you'd better change your tune. I daresay our friends and acquaintances will be having a good laugh at your expense.'

'Yours too!' she flashed at him.

He shook his head. 'We won't bore Katrina with all the details, but no one is going to laugh at me.' He strolled over to the drinks tray. 'What are you drinking?'

'Gin and tonic.' Virginia threw a defiant look at Katrina. 'A large one.'

Katrina ignored the look; she thought Virginia drank a little too much, but now was hardly the time to say so. She looked vague and sipped her sherry.

'Well,' asked Lucius briskly, 'have the wedding arrangements been made? I'll give you away with pleasure.'

Katrina said sharply: 'Now, Lucius!' and went on calmly: 'There's Uncle Wallace in Peterborough . . . or Uncle James—but he's in Scotland.'

'Oh, anyone will do,' declared Virginia. 'As though anyone will notice. Katrina, I'm going up to town tomorrow to see about my dress—I shall want heaps of money, and I don't want to be bothered with all the arrangements. I'll see about the bridesmaids, but you can see to the rest.'

'I'll need to know which day,' said Katrina.

'Oh, the Hunt Ball is at the end of next week, isn't it? The week after that—Tuesday will do.'

'Isn't James interested in knowing the date?' asked Lucius.

'I'll give him a ring. We're going abroad afterwards and we shan't come back until the end of January. James's mother is going to move into the old rectory—it's been empty for months.'

'Won't she mind?' asked Katrina.

Virginia turned her lovely eyes on to her. 'I've no idea. But I won't have her in the house, bossing me around.'

Katrina let that pass. James's mother was a mouse of a little woman, who spoiled him utterly and would never dream of going against his wishes. She said doubtfully: 'I hope you'll be happy.'

'I shall be rich,' said Virginia smugly.

It was on the tip of Katrina's tongue to remind her that if she had married Lucius she would have been richer, but she caught his eye in time and kept quiet.

'You owe Katrina an apology,' said Lucius presently. 'You said a great many stupid and hurtful things about her, the least you can do is say you're sorry.'

Virginia stood up. 'But I'm not sorry, and I hope everyone laughs themselves sick—the idea of you and Lucius fancying each other!' She began to laugh. 'What are you going to do about it?'

'As to that,' said Lucius blandly, 'you must wait and see, mustn't you?' He glanced at Katrina, sitting very composed but rather pale. 'Are you going to the Vicarage this evening, Katie?'

She said that yes, she was, and Virginia gave a little crow of laughter. 'What a thrill!' she declared.

'You've been asked too,' Katrina reminded her quietly.

'Well, I'm not going—you can make some excuse . . .'

'No, if you don't want to go you can make your own excuses.' She nodded towards the phone. 'You'd better do it now.'

Virginia shrugged. 'O.K., though I do think it's rotten of you.' She dialled a number and they listened to her excusing herself from the evening's entertainment with charm and ingenuity. When she'd finished she went to the door. 'I'm going over to see the Frobishers; they'll want to be bridesmaids.' She didn't say goodbye.

'You need another drink,' said Lucius, and sat down again. 'I'll call for you about half past seven—and wear the brown thing.'

'Don't call it a thing!'

He took no notice of her indignant interruption: 'And you must go back to that boutique and get something for the wedding.'

'I'm quite able to buy my own clothes.'

'You always look very nice, Katie,' said Lucius smoothly, 'but left to your own devices you'll choose something neat and navy blue. I shall come with you.'

They went to the dining room and started their lunch, and as soon as Lovelace had gone, Katrina said: 'It's the bride's day—she has to outshine everyone.'

'I have no doubt that Virginia will manage that; it's one of her aims in an aimless life, isn't it?'

'Didn't you love her at all, Lucius?'

'Not at all,' he told her coolly.

'Then why . . .'

'You asked me to wean her from the countless young men flocking round her. She isn't my type, Katie.'

It was on the tip of her tongue to ask what his type was, but she had never poked her nose into his private life and she wasn't going to start now. It was disconcerting when he said softly: 'Quite right, my dear, don't ask.'

'Well, I wasn't going to. As a matter of fact,' she added carefully, 'I'm not in the least interested.' She uttered the lie in a matter-of-fact voice which didn't deceive Lucius in the least.

'Have you heard from Mrs Lovell?' he wanted to know as they drank their coffee. 'Has young Lovell been to see you—or phoned?'

'No.' Katrina tried to look assured and failed. 'Should I have?'

'Why not ring Mrs Lovell? If Virginia wants this wedding when she says she does, there's not much time to lose.'

Which meant that, eagerly bidden to call that very afternoon by the mouselike Mrs Lovell,

Katrina found herself in the Jaguar, being driven to that lady's house.

The Lovells' home was of comfortable size in its own large grounds and furnished splendidly; there was no lack of money, indeed, Mrs Lovell had been left very well off and James had money of his own; Virginia would be able to indulge her every whim. Lucius stopped before the entrance porch and got out with Katrina. He glanced up at the front of the house. 'Our Virginia has done quite well for herself,' he observed, and rang the bell.

Mrs Lovell was glad to see them. 'I wasn't sure if I should telephone you!' she said worriedly. 'James is putting the notice in the papers today, and he said there'd be nothing for me to do but attend the wedding.'

'Guests?' asked Lucius gently.

'Yes. Oh well—perhaps we could make a list. It's to be at Upper Tew, isn't it? James says Virginia wants a big wedding; they're coming here this evening, I believe—but the church won't hold any more than two hundred, will it? And where will you hold the reception?'

'At home,' said Katrina composedly, her mind racing round in circles—buffet lunch, and Old John would be furious if he had to use all his precious plants from the glasshouse. 'Could we make a quick list of guests now and ask Virginia and James to add anyone else this evening? Then we could get them away tomorrow—it's very short notice, but it can't be helped.' She frowned. 'I'll get the caterers on to it tomorrow once we've a rough idea of how many there'll be.'

Mrs Lovell, smiling uncertainly, said: 'It's all quite a rush, isn't it? I knew that James was fond of Virginia, of course . . .' her eyes slid to Lucius and she went slowly red. He smiled at her. 'But the best man always wins, doesn't he?' He didn't appear in the least put out and in a moment she smiled too. 'It's all very suitable,' she murmured.

The lists were made over a cup of tea, with Lucius obligingly writing them down and totting up the names. 'Sixty for Katrina, seventy for you, Mrs Lovell, which leaves seventy for the happy couple to split between them.' He handed them each the lists of names. 'I'm going up to town tomorrow, if you like to draft out the invitation cards I'll take them along to a printers.'

Mrs Lovell was effusive in her thanks, Katrina less so. Lucius was behaving—for a man who had been treated as Virginia had treated him—in a most untypical manner, for all the world as though he were the brother or even the father of the bride. She threw him a suspicious glance and met his grey eyes, usually so cool but now gleaming with amusement.

'You seem very anxious to get Virginia married,' she observed as they drove back.

'I like to clear the decks ready for action,' was all he said. She sat and puzzled that one out, and came to no conclusion at all. He dropped her at her own door and drove back to his home, with the reminder that he would be back for her at half past seven.

Katrina took great pains with her appearance, and was rewarded by Lucius's 'very nice', when he called for her. He was wearing a dark grey suit and a rather splendid tie; he looked handsome, interesting, and wore the bland expression which told her nothing at all. As she got into the car beside him he observed: 'There may be a little awkwardness, though I'm sure we can depend upon Mr Moffat to smooth things over.' He glanced sideways at her. 'you look more than a match for anyone.'

She wasn't sure if he meant that or if he was just being kind. 'Yes, but what am I going to say?' she asked in a panic.

'You'll think of something,' he told her comfortably.

All the same, her head was empty as they went into the Rectory's drawing room—an apartment of Victorian vastness which was only half filled by the eight people already in it. She knew them all, of course, and went around greeting them with the warmth of long acquaintance. It was Mrs Turner, the doctor's wife, who drew her a little on one side. 'My dear,' she began, 'Virginia told us such an extraordinary story—is it a joke? Is she really marrying James Lovell—I quite thought . . .' Her eyes swivelled round to where Lucius was standing. 'You know she and Lucius—they've been in each other's pockets for weeks.'

Mrs Moffat had sidled up to join them. Katrina took a breath. 'Just good friends,' she said calmly, 'while she was making up her mind about James.'

'But, my dear,' chimed in Mrs Moffat, 'she said such peculiar things! No one would believe them, of course—not that she wasn't speaking the truth, but I daresay she was overwrought . . . a young girl,' she added vaguely.

'But of course it's nonsense,' declared Mrs Turner. 'I mean, you and Lucius—you've known each other since you were in prams!'

Katrina couldn't quite see why two babies in their prams shouldn't grow up and fall in love and marry if they felt so inclined, but she didn't say so because that might have put ideas in her companions' heads. She remembered with a spark of rage that Lucius had other ideas, and wondered what he was saying. It was impossible to find out; he was at the other end of the room, talking to Dr Turner.

The evening seemed to go on for ever. The wedding was the main topic of conversation, of course, at least among the ladies. 'You'll find that house of yours rather large when Virginia's gone,' observed Mrs Moffat kindly, and Lucius, standing close by, had turned his head and said pleasantly: 'Probably she won't be there very long, Mrs Moffat.' He had smiled brilliantly at Katrina as he spoke and she had blushed scarlet. If looks could have killed, he would have dropped dead where he stood!

It was on their way home that she demanded furiously: 'Why did you have to say that? Now everyone is wondering . . .'

His tone was infuriatingly matter-of-fact. 'But we want them to, don't we? If Virginia amused herself spreading wild rumours about us, we might as well give them credence.' He came to a halt outside her front door and turned to look at her. 'And there's no need for you to be so peevish about it—I told you I was going to court you.'

Katrina tried to open the door and couldn't. 'You are impossible,' she told him. 'All this silly talk!'

'I rather like the term myself—it has a nice honest ring to it, like walking out. Which reminds me, you'd better come up to town with me tomorrow and get clothes. You'll have to live to a tight schedule from now on.'

He got out of the car and opened the door for her. 'Do you suppose your Mrs Beecham will have any of her soup lying around in the kitchen? Mrs Moffat is a dear soul, but I never get enough to eat when we go there to dine.'

Katrina said crossly: 'Oh, come inside, do,' and swept past him into the hall where Lovelace was advancing to meet them. 'Lovelace, Mr Massey is hungry—he wants some soup.'

Lovelace beamed at them both. 'There now, miss, Mrs Beecham left a saucepan of her special mushroom soup on the stove, seeing that it's such a cold night. I'll fetch it along.'

Lucius had flung his coat on to a chair. 'Let's have it in the kitchen.' He looked at Lovelace. 'We can help ourselves—you were locking up, I expect.'

'Well, really,' said Katrina coldly as they went to the kitchen, 'anyone would think this was your house—the cheek of it!'

She swept to the old-fashioned dresser and got two soup bowls with a good deal of noise.

'My dear soul, I've been in and out of your kitchen since I could toddle, but since you insist, I'll just sit at the table and you shall serve the soup.'

'Oh, be quiet, do!' said Katrina abruptly. 'You seem to find everything so amusing—it was a beastly evening, and you made it worse. And you can get your own soup!'

'Better that that, I'll get yours as well. Where's the bread?'

He called for her at half past eight the next morning; she had told herself that she had no intention of going with him, but he had coolly worn her down and here she was, sitting beside him once more, warmly wrapped up against the cold morning. She hadn't seen Virginia, although

Lovelace had told her that she had come in very late on the previous night. She left a message that she would be back that evening and begged Virginia to add the names of any guests she wanted to the list she had left on her desk. In the car she said worriedly: 'I wonder why Virginia was so late home? It was past two o'clock, Lovelace told me.'

Lucius laughed. 'My dear Katrina, if you were engaged to be married, with the date fixed and a large diamond ring on your finger, where do you suppose you'd be?'

She said huffily: 'You're just guessing. Besides . . .'

He slid past a slow-moving van. 'The young today have rather different ideas from us older ones.' His voice was bland and held a hint of laughter.

'Don't make me sound middle-aged!' said Katrina indignantly. 'I'm not thirty yet.'

'Exactly, that's why we're on our way to buy your outfit for the wedding—left to yourself you would come home with something in excellent taste, beige or grey and guaranteed to dim your radiance.'

She was uncertain about the radiance, but in bed that night she had to admit that if she had been shopping on her own, she would never have bought an outfit in old rose silk, nor would she have chosen a wide-brimmed hat of leghorn straw trimmed with pink roses. 'I shall be so conspicuous!' she almost wailed at Lucius as they travelled back to Upper Tew.

And all he had said was: 'You'll look exactly as you're supposed to look.'

She looked at the outfit, hanging beside the new

ball dresses the next morning before she started to dress; they looked out of place beside the sober garments about them. Not knowing why she should do so, she chose a pleated skirt in a sensible shade of brown and topped it with a cream silk blouse and a thick sweater just as sensible.

The Hunt Ball was at the end of the week, and beyond one or two committee meetings in the village, planning Christmas parties for the school children and an outing for the very elderly, Katrina had nothing much to do. Which was as well, because organising the wedding was taking all her spare time, although it was wonderful what money could do, she thought. The invitation cards were printed with speed, the caterers had everything tied up within an hour or so, extra help was found in the village, the bridesmaids agreed with heartening speed about their dresses, and the florist at Chipping Sodbury was only too glad to provide the flowers.

Virginia had wanted them sent down from London, but Katrina had been firm about this. 'Suppose there's a hitch and they don't arrive?' she wanted to know. She had spoken sharply because Virginia spent so much time away from home and expected all the arrangements to be made at the drop of a hat and with no trouble to herself. She had hardly spoken to Katrina, and certainly went out of her way to ignore Lucius. Which wasn't surprising; both he and Katrina had had their fill of veiled questions and friendly jokes.

The weather turned bitterly cold and there was a thin icing of snow on the morning of the Hunt Ball. Katrina hadn't seen anything of Lucius for two days and supposed him to be away and Virginia and James, who had come to lunch had driven off again, presumably to his home. Katrina had been there again, this time driving herself, to confer with Mrs Lovell, and that lady had been to lunch with her, but any help Katrina might have expected from her wasn't forthcoming. Beyond waffling on and on about her wedding outfit, Mrs Lovell had nothing constructive to say. Katrina had wished heartily that Lucius had been with them to help the conversation along. Alone in the house, she washed her hair, then wrapped herself up and took Bouncer for a brisk walk. As she came back down the lane she could see lights shining from Stockley House and the Jaguar was standing on the sweep before the front of the house. Lucius was home.

The green dress, so unlike anything she had ever worn before, certainly became her. She stood in front of the pier-glass, studying her image, and for once was satisfied. True, she wished for curling hair, regular features, several inches more height and tapering white hands instead of the small capable ones she possessed, albeit beautifully kept, but since she had none of them, she decided that Lucius had been right; the dress suited her.

She picked up the chinchilla coat her father had given her for her twenty-first birthday, checked her purse, and went downstairs. Lovelace had brought her car round to the door for her and she got in and drove the short distance to Stockley House.

Cobb admitted her, took her coat and led her to the drawing room where Lucius was entertaining his dinner guests. The room was fairly full despite its size and he was at the farther end of it, but he excused himself as she went in and crossed the carpeted floor to meet her. Which meant that everyone there stopped their chatter to look at her.

Lucius bent to kiss her cheek. 'Quite an entrance, my dear,' he said softly. 'That's an enchanting dress.'

She was conscious of disappointment because althought he had admired her dress he hadn't actually admired her. There was, she considered, quite a difference—but there was no time to split hairs. She began a leisurely tour of the room, greeting everyone there; she had known most of them all her life.

Lucius could be very grand when occasion demanded. The table sparkled with family silver and magnificent glass; the Spode china echoed the colours of the centrepiece—gold and bronze and white. Katrina found herself near him between Sir William Jermyn, who owned most of the land on the other side of the village, and young Peter Crawley, who lived for his hunting and had little interest in anything else. Katrina, who disliked it very much although she was keen enough on riding, listened politely to the latest news of the hunting field and then applied herself to her elderly partner on the other side, who collected Fulda figures—they were rare enough to cause him to travel in their search, and since he was just back from Fulda where he had acquired a specially fine piece, he had a good deal to say. Katrina listened to him as politely as she had to Peter Crawley and ate the excellent dinner Lucius had provided, but she was glad though to go into the drawing room with the other women and have her coffee, although she hadn't expected quite so much interest in herself.

She had been prepared to answer questions about the wedding, because everyone there had been invited, anyway, but after several pleasing comments upon her appearance the questions became a little more difficult to answer. What were her own plans for the future? Would she be spending Christmas at home or perhaps at Stockley House? Someone had seen them dining at La Sorbonne and wanted to know, rather archly, if she and Lucius enjoyed going out together. It was a good thing that the men joined them very shortly and everyone dispersed to drive to Maudell House, ten miles away, where the Ball was to be held. She did her best to make herself inconspicuous as they all gathered in the hall, offering lifts to each other, but Lucius caught her arm and said loudly: 'Of course you'll come with me, Katie,' giving her a smile so full of charm that several of the older ladies standing near sighed sentimentally and exchanged meaningful glances.

The ball was well attended. It took Katrina some time to discover Virginia and James, dancing together. They made a splendid couple, and Virginia's dress was stunning. Katrina danced with Lucius and then with a succession of men, all of whom complimented her on her appearance, some of them with faint surprise in their voices, and when she danced with Lucius again he observed: 'You're going down very well, Katie—even stealing some of Virginia's thunder.'

'I don't want to do that,' she protested. 'She's the bride-to-be!'

He raised his eyebrows. 'Ah, yes, but everyone here expects you to be the next one.' He grinned suddenly. 'Several of our more elderly friends have expressed the opinion that we shall make a very good match, you and I.'

'You never let them think that? Just to annoy Virginia? Lucius, how could you?'

'Easily, especially as it's true. Really you are the most unresponsive girl, Katie! Here I am, courting you for all it's worth, and you refuse to take me seriously.' He tightened his hold on her. 'And don't look so furious—do try to remember that I've been completely won over by your brains, elegance and knowledge of the world.'

Katrina giggled, then said: 'But it's not funny really. I'm not any of those things and it's absurd to suggest it.'

'Perhaps.' He stared down at her, his eyes amused although he looked serious. 'In any case I prefer you as you are, just Katie.'

He didn't dance with her again for quite a while. The noise and crush of people, indicative of the success of the evening, got worse and worse and finally ended in a wild gallop round and round the ballroom. Katrina, who had been partnering Peter Crawley, suddenly found that he had gone and that Lucius was there instead—a great improvement, she decided, whirling along at a great rate. Lucius was large, heavily built and acted nicely as a buffer between her and wildly rushing dancers round her. The whole thing ended with everyone almost too breathless to sing 'God Save the Queen'.

'The best ball we've had for a long time,' remarked Katrina, being edged towards the ladies' cloakroom—a converted bedroom at the top of the wide staircase. The Frobishers were struggling to the top too.

'And next year I suppose you'll be married,' said the eldest Frobisher girl. 'It's all very romantic, Katrina. We should never have guessed about you and Lucius—I mean, Virginia told us all that she and . . .'

To Katrina's relief someone pushed between them and she edged away. It was two o'clock in the morning and she was far too tired to give the right answers. Bother Lucius, she thought crossly, searching for her coat in the huge piles around the room. She found it presently and went back to the hall and saw him waiting goodnaturedly while his party sorted themselves out for the drive back to Stockley House. When the last guest had squeezed into the last car he took her arm, settled her in the Jaguar, waved a final goodbye to their host and hostess, and drove off. It was a cold clear night with a thick frost. Katrina could see the tail lights of the cars ahead of them going up the hill outside the village; they made the sleeping country around them seem lonely.

'Nice evening,' observed Lucius, and she agreed sleepily, then added: 'Except for that last bit, getting our coats. I got asked a lot of silly questions.'

'About us?' She could hear the laughter in his voice.

'Yes.'

'Good.' And before she could reply to that: 'Come riding after breakfast? Half past nine?' He took it for granted that she would agree. 'Everything fixed up for the wedding?'

'More or less. But I've too much to do to come riding . . .'

'You'll do it all the better for fresh air and exercise.' They had caught up with the other cars and he had slowed down.

She said sleepily: 'Lucius, I do feel we're in the most frightful muddle.'

'No, we're not. Look, concentrate on the

wedding and let everything else slide for the moment.'

'Yes, that's all very well—you're only doing it to get even with Virginia, aren't you?'

They were in front of the house—her house—and he turned off the engine and turned to look at her. She couldn't see how cold his eyes were, which was a good thing. 'I know what I'm doing, Katrina.'

He got out and opened her door and saw her safely indoors, then with the briefest of goodnights, went away.

CHAPTER FOUR

IT was a heavenly morning; cold and frosty and clear skies. Katrina was up soon after eight o'clock, and after a solitary breakfast, went down to the stables. There was no sign of Virginia, but she hadn't expected to see her before midday and she had told Mrs Beecham to let her sleep undisturbed. She was saddling her mare when Lucius arrived, and he got off his own horse and finished the job for her, before leading the way down the drive and along the lane and through his own gates again.

'I have to see Stevens about that barn of his; we'll cut across the ten-acre field and take a look at Chivett's cottage—the thatch is wearing badly.'

It was exhilarating, going fast over the hard ground. Katrina rode well and Lucius gave her a look of approval as they went. He rode well himself, sitting his great horse with ease, holding him in to keep pace with Katrina's mare.

They hardly spoke; they had ridden together for years now, content with each other's company, talking when they felt inclined. When they reached Chivett's cottage they dismounted, tied the horses to the gate post and went inside. Chivett was old, a retired gamekeeper who had worked for Lucius's father. A middle-aged widowed daughter looked after him, and although he was really crippled with rheumatism now, he refused to do anything about it. His daughter made them welcome, poured

stewed tea from an enamelled pot and then took
Katrina off to see the hens while Lucius talked to
the old man. That was something nice about him,
thought Katrina, treading the path behind the
cottage behind her hostess. He minded about his
property and the people who worked for him.
There was no need to discuss the thatch with old
Chivett, but it wouldn't enter Lucius's head not to
do so; the old man would be left with the pleasant
impression that he had given advice about it to
young Mr Lucius, whereas anyone else might have
had the roof repaired without so much as a word
to him. She admired the hens and went back to
find Lucius waiting for her.

The visit to Stevens farm took longer. They were
given more tea, asked about the Hunt Ball, and
presently Lucius went away to inspect the barn
and Katrina was left with Mrs Stevens, a nice cosy
dumpling of a woman.

They had known each other a long while. They
talked about the children, the farm, Mrs Stevens'
various mild ailments and the weather before Mrs
Stevens said comfortably: 'There'll be the wedding
next week, then. Church'll be full, I daresay. Miss
Virginia'll make a lovely bride. I did hear that it
was Mister Lucius as she was going to marry,
though mark you, there's always gossip in a
village. Never believed it, myself.' Her mild blue
eyes searched Katrina's quiet face. 'He'll wed when
he's ready, and I doubt he's already sure in his
mind who it'll be.'

'Well, yes, I daresay,' agreed Katrina. 'Are you
coming to the wedding?' They talked of nothing
else until the two men came back, and presently
she and Lucius said goodbye and rode off.

Lucius refused her invitation to stay for lunch

and she didn't see him for several days. She told herself that this was a good thing, because she was busy enough with last-minute preparations and James seemed to be in the house for almost twenty-four hours of the day. That he was very much in love was evident, and as far as Katrina could see, her sister was in love with him. He had showered her with gifts, all of which she had accepted as her due, but with a charming grace, and although she avoided Katrina her behaviour wasn't to be faulted when they were together. True, she did nothing to help with the preparations for the wedding. Her dress was delivered, there were sessions with the bridesmaids to make sure that their outfits were exactly as she wanted them, and a rehearsal at the church which Katrina didn't attend.

The wedding morning dawned clear and cold and Katrina, getting dressed for the ceremony, wondered if she had made a mistake, choosing rose-coloured silk, even though it was a heavy material, and a straw hat, in midwinter. True, the hat had a lining to its brim of palest pink velvet and the rose was velvet, which made it rather more wintry, and the colour suited her and went well with her chinchilla coat. When she was ready she went along to Virginia's room. Sitting composedly in front of her dressing table, her sister looked exquisite, and Katrina said so.

'And what's come over *you*?' asked Virginia. 'I expected you to wear brown or navy blue or dove grey.' Her beautiful eyes narrowed. 'I bet Lucius chose that outfit!'

'Well, he was with me when I bought it. I'm changing my image.' Katrina added reasonably: 'I can't do anything else after the things you said about me, can I? Shall I go along and see if the bridesmaids are ready? It's almost time to leave. Uncle is in the sitting room—I'll warn him I'm going now.'

She crossed the room and stooped to kiss Virginia's cheek. 'I hope you'll both be very happy, darling.'

Virginia didn't answer, only laughed a little, and as Katrina opened the door, she asked: 'Don't you wish you were me, Katie?' She laughed again. 'Of course, you can always marry Lucius!'

The last thing she would do, thought Katrina, being driven in state to the church.

The pews were crammed. It wasn't a very large church to begin with, and now, over and above the guests, as many local people as possible had packed themselves into it. Katrina was ushered to her seat at the front, smiling at the people she knew, very conscious that Lucius was sitting directly behind her. She sat serenely, wondering if her hair was all right at the back and quite shattered when Lucius breathed in her ear: 'Relax, Katie, you look delightful.'

She managed not to turn round; she was aware of the heads turned in her direction and went pink so that the heads nodded to each other and exchanged knowing smiles. Luckily the organ swelled and the bride, a little late, started on her way down the aisle.

The wedding went off very well. The bride looked exquisite and so did the bridesmaids, the happy couple made their responses in clear voices, the choir sang angelically and Mr Moffat, quite carried away by the occasion, gave a moving address. No one listened to it, of course. The ladies were busy pricing each other's hats and the men wondering what food there would be later on. Presently they went to the vestry to sign the register and then proceeded down the aisle to the organist's vigorous rendering of the Wedding March. Katrina, beside a distant cousin she hadn't seen for years, felt the beginnings of a headache. If ever I marry, which isn't likely, she thought, I'll have the quietest wedding imaginable, a velvet suit and one of those small hats that look as though they're tied at the back, and no bridesmaids . . . The cousin nipped her arm sharply; she had never liked him, now she gave him a vexed look.

'They're going to take photos,' he hissed. 'You could at least look interested!'

Back at the house, she and Mrs Lovell stood side by side, receiving the guests with the bride and bridegroom; endless kissing and hand-shaking and a startling number of whispered: 'I expect you'll be the next, Katrina,' from the older ladies. Old Lady Ryder, never one to lower her voice, bellowed: 'I've always said you'd make a better wife for Lucius than that young sister of yours—she'd have been too young!'

Katrina, her cheeks the colour of her dress, stitched a smile on to her face and murmured, aware that Lucius, standing not too far away, had heard every word—as had almost everyone there.

People began to circulate presently and find their way to the dining room where a buffet had been set up and then wander on into the sitting room, where there were small tables arranged to accommodate them; it was surprising how easily the old house absorbed so many people. Katrina heaved a sigh of satisfaction, took the champagne Lovelace was offering and tossed it off, quite forgetting that she had had almost no breakfast that morning, but it made her feel good, and as he went past again she put her empty glass on the tray and took another, to find Lucius at her elbow with a plate of vol-au-vents.

'I'm not hungry', she told him airily.

'Well, they wouldn't be much use if you were,' he conceded. 'Have one all the same. What are you doing this evening?'

'Going to bed early,' she said promptly.

'Good idea, but before you do I'll come over for you. You can eat at my place, it'll give your people a chance to get things straight.'

She took a slurp of champagne. 'I thought . . .' she began, and caught his eye. 'Well, it would be nice—there'll be a lot to do even if the catering people clear up after them. But oughtn't I stay and help?'

'No, have another of these things.'

She took one reluctantly. 'I'm thirsty,' she complained. 'I'd love a cup of tea.'

'You shall have one presently.' He was standing in front of her, blocking her view, and now he looked round him. 'Everyone seems to be enjoying themselves; they'll be cutting the cake soon. I must say there's an impressive display of presents.'

'Lovelace and I were up half the night putting them out. Virginia said not to bother, but people get hurt . . . What did you give them? I didn't see anything.'

'An impressive and quite hideous épergne, solid silver and guaranteed to take up the entire centre of the dining room table. I shall expect to see it when I'm bidden to dine with them.'

Katrina finished her champagne and giggled. 'I should like some more champagne,' she said, and gave him her empty glass.

'And so you shall, but don't you think you should make a trip round the guests first? I'll be here waiting.' He smiled down at her. 'Champagne and roses—I had no idea you had it in you, Katie.'

'What do you mean?'

'I'll tell you later. Go and do your duty, there's a good girl.'

Once she got started it didn't seem like duty. It was amazing what a couple of glasses of champagne did for her. She went from group to group, laughing and chatting with such sparkle that everyone there who hadn't quite believed Virginia's story found themselves having second thoughts. Katrina in her pink outfit was quite a different kettle of fish from the rather quiet, tweed clad girl they all knew. It was amazing what love did to a girl, whispered Lady Ryder *sotto voce*. Katrina, while never pretty, was decidedly striking. 'These quiet ones are deep,' she boomed, and Katrina, hearing her, looked enquiring.

'We are discussing the Italian Lakes,' observed Mrs Turner hastily, in a panic in case Lady Ryder should flatly contradict her. Indeed, the old lady had her mouth open to do so when the toastmaster prayed silence and Katrina slipped back to where Lucius was waiting for her.

He handed her her drink without a word. 'And don't gulp it all down, we'll be starting on the toasts at any minute.'

The speeches took a long time, but finally the cake was cut, more toasts were drunk and the bride, accompanied by a flurry of bridesmaids, went away to change. Katrina, suddenly famished, ate two éclairs, several cocktail sausages, a chicken and mushroom bouchée and a cheese tartlet—not all at once, of course; she had to time her forays between conversations with her guests. These morsels merely sharpened her appetite, though, and when she bumped into Lucius she said a trifle wildly: 'Tea and hot buttered toast—that's all I want.'

'You shall have them as soon as everyone's gone. An hour at the most.'

He was as good as his word. The bride and groom seen on their way by a shower of confetti, the guests began to leave until finally there were only Mrs Lovell and a handful of her family left; and presently they went too. Katrina waved them goodbye from the steps and the moment the car was out of sight took off her hat and kicked off her shoes. Lucius was still there, of course, but she was used to him being about the house and she would have found it strange if he had gone home too. He picked up her shoes and hat, laid them neatly on a chair and took her arm.

'Tea and toast,' he reminded her, and when she hesitated: 'Don't worry, everyone's going to have half an hour's break before starting on the tidying up.'

The place looked a shambles—plates of food, untold glasses, screwed up paper serviettes, ash trays, bottles, plates and an assortment of forgotten gloves, but Lovelace had cleared a space round the fire in the sitting room and set a tea tray on a small table nearby. Katrina curled up in a chair, begged Lovelace to give himself and everyone else an hour's peace and quiet and poured the tea. There was buttered toast in a covered dish. She lifted the lid and offered it to Lucius.

He shook his head. 'I won't stop, Katie. Enjoy your tea—I'll be back for you at half past seven.'

He waved a casual hand and went away, letting himself out and closing the great house door gently behind him. Katrina heard the Jaguar's engine as he started up and drove away. She had expected him to stay. Tired though she was, it would have been fun to have mulled over the day with someone. She bit into her toast and wondered why he'd gone away so abruptly. She had wanted to talk to him anyway; it was time an end was put to his ridiculous notion—Virginia had behaved badly, but she was married now; everyone would forget, and in a month or two she would return and life would go on as usual, and their friends would remember the silly joke about herself and Lucius and laugh a little and then forget all about it.

She dropped off into a doze and woke presently to find Lovelace taking away the tea tray, and when she asked him if they could cope with the clearing up he said soothingly: 'Oh, yes, Miss Katrina, we've all had a good tea and a sit down and Mr Lucius has sent over Bolt and Jane to give a hand; we shall be back to normal by this evening.'

Bolt and Jane were the gardener and the housemaid at Stockley House and good friends of Lovelace and Mrs Beecham. Katrina said: 'That was very thoughtful of Mr Lucius. I'm going there to dinner, Lovelace, so Mrs Beecham won't need to cook anything for me. Have a good supper yourselves, won't you?'

She went upstairs and did her face and hair and then, armed with a bottle or two, went to the kitchen and thanked everyone there for making the day such a success. 'You all worked so hard.' She put an envelope on the table beside the bottles

and addressed the three caterers' staff. 'Please get
yourself a drink—you were splendid.'

She smiled at them all and went back to the
sitting room to wait for Lucius. He came
punctually, and when she saw that he had changed
from his morning dress to a dark grey suit she
said: 'I haven't changed—I hope you don't mind. I
went to sleep and didn't have time.'

'I'm glad. I like you in that pink outfit, and you
must know, my dear, that a man only wears
morning dress when he's forced to. If you are
ready we'll go.'

Lovelace had appeared silent-footed in the hall.
He opened the door for them with a fatherly smile,
wished them a pleasant evening and assured
Katrina that he would wait up for her.

'Well, she won't be late, Lovelace,' declared
Lucius, 'she's half asleep already.' It was the sort
of unflattering remark which he made so often
that she took no notice of it, and Lovelace, who
had covered up for them on many a youthful
escapade, merely inclined his elderly head in a
dignified way and murmured, 'Quite so, Mr
Lucius.'

They didn't talk on the short drive to Stockley
House, but once there, sitting comfortably by the
fire in the drawing-room, Katrina said: 'We have
to have a talk—a sensible one, Lucius—none of
your ridiculous ideas. Everyone has got it all wrong
about us, and you've got to help me explain . . .'

'Explain what?' he asked silkily.

'You know quite well—all this nonsense about
us . . . the things Virginia said. Today at the
reception I was asked . . .' She paused, a little
daunted by the look of bland amusement on his
face. 'You know quite well what I was asked,' she

finished crossly, 'so don't pretend you don't. We have to put a stop to it.'

'I've always considered you a clear-headed girl, Katie, but it seems I've been wrong. Didn't I tell you we're walking out together? Indeed, I've made no efforts to disprove this among our many friends and acquaintances.'

Katrina sat up with a jerk. 'But, Lucius, why? It's all over and done with now.' Her beautiful brown eyes flashed with sudden temper. 'I didn't think you were so small-minded!'

He only smiled at her, took her glass and refilled it and sat down again. 'How long is it now since we've known each other?' he asked.

She looked at him in surprise. 'Well, I'm twenty-seven, and I suppose you saw me in my pram— you'd have been seven years old.'

'And you would say we've been good friends during those years?' He added with faint mockery: 'Until I broke Virginia's heart.'

She said gruffly: 'Well, you know we have.'

'And do you really suppose I would allow a friend of such long standing—as close—no, closer—than a sister, to be ridiculed by her sister, even if it was meant as a bad joke and no one really believed it?'

Katrina stared at him, drank her sherry at one gulp and said in a small voice: 'You mean you . . . I thought you were pretending it was true so that you could get even with Virginia.'

He raised his eyebrows. 'My dear girl, I've never wished to get even with anyone; but since, according to Virginia, I've been—er—bowled over by your brains and elegance, and what was the other thing? Ah, yes, knowledge of the world, and not forgetting your maturity, then let our friends assume that that is the case.'

'Yes, but it's not, is it? I mean, we can't go on for ever walking out.'

'Of course not, that would be too tedious, it sounds to me to be a very straitlaced procedure. We'll work our way by easy stages to a vague engagement and by then everyone will have lost interest.' He broke off as Cobb came to tell them that dinner was served, and during the meal Lucius kept up a gentle flow of small talk which took them pleasantly through the delicious consommé, the fried whitebait, the duck with brandy, pineapple and curaçao and the mince tart with clotted cream. Katrina, feeling much more herself after such good food and with two glasses of Lucius's best hock inside her, turned a much less jaundiced eye on the situation.

Back in the drawing room, pouring coffee from the George the Second coffee pot, she said suddenly: 'Well, it's very kind of you, Lucius, and I feel very mean about it, because I didn't realise ... that is, I thought you were pretending just to please yourself. Won't it be a bore for you?'

His face was in shadow and she couldn't see it very clearly, but his voice was reassuringly matter-of-fact. 'Why should it bore me? We've always seen a great deal of each other, all we have to do is spend an evening in town from time to time and take care to be seen together in public. Besides, I'd planned to go to Greece for a week or two after Christmas—you can come too—in fact, you'll have to, otherwise people will think I've jilted you as well as Virginia.'

'Greece?' Katrina's voice came out a surprised squeak, she said the first thing which came to her head. 'But I haven't any clothes ...'

'Then we can spend a pleasant day in town buying whatever you need.'

She said crossly: 'You've always had an answer to everything, Lucius. So soon after Christmas,' she grumbled.

'There couldn't be a better time. Your staff can have a few weeks' holiday. We won't be here when James and Virginia come back from their honeymoon—and that might be a good thing. You'll come here for Christmas Day, of course. The usual aunts and uncles and cousins will be here—you can help me entertain them.'

She said feebly: 'I'd planned a quiet few days . . .'

'Out of the question. Have a drinks party on Christmas Eve if you want to, and come here for Christmas Day and Boxing Day.'

'You've got it all nicely arranged,' Katrina said feebly.

'Naturally these things need to be planned ahead. You surely didn't think you'd spend Christmas alone?'

'Well, I had thought I'd have a few people in for a drink—we always have done, you know.' She added defiantly: 'I thought I'd like a quiet time to myself.'

'In theory yes, in practice, no. Tomorrow we'll go and tell Lovelace and Mrs Beecham what we've decided.'

'But I've not decided anything,' she said with a flash of spirit. 'Don't bully me, Lucius!'

'Dear girl, if I didn't bully you, you'd sit here alone, dressed in navy blue or beige, only going out when bidden, and then in a garment which shrouded your still youthful charms from neck to ankle.'

'I'm twenty-seven,' she told him bleakly.

'And I'm thirty-four. We have all our lives before us, my dear. You'll spend Christmas here and we'll go together to Greece.' He smiled at her with great gentleness. 'When you were a little girl, you never questioned anything I suggested. Don't do it now.'

'I've never been to Greece,' said Katrina slowly.

'Athens, I thought, and Cape Sounion where we'll get a fine view of the Aegean Islands. I'll hire a car and we can go farther afield. There should be plenty of sun and it will be pleasantly warm.'

'It sounds interesting.'

'Good, I'll get the tickets—some time in early January.'

He took her home presently, seeing her through her own front door and wishing her a casual goodnight. It was still quite early. Katrina told Lovelace to lock up and went to bed, falling asleep almost as soon as her head touched the pillow.

The next day was totally taken up with getting the house back to normal, packing up the wedding presents to be taken over to the Lovells' house, and making plans for Christmas, and in the evening after dinner she sat at her desk, writing the Christmas cards and making a list of friends who should come for drinks. It was a lengthy business and once or twice she found herself wishing Lucius might come in and chat for half an hour. But there was no sign of him, nor the next day, either.

One day after that she got up earlier than usual, took Bouncer for a walk, had breakfast and went up to the Studio. There was the book jacket to get started on; she did some rough sketches, not content with any of them, and was sitting staring at them when the door opened and Lucius walked in.

'Up early, aren't you? I saw you out with Bouncer hours ago. If you've nothing better to do we'll go up to town and do some shopping.'

Katrina eyed him coolly. 'I thought I'd get on with this—they want it before the New Year.'

He came and peered over her shoulder. 'Don't you like any of them? I don't. A change of scene will help. Go and put on a coat. I'll take you to lunch and you can help me choose the crackers for the school party.'

She hesitated. The village school was something everyone bothered about; so far they had hung on to it, despite Authority's ideas about sending the children to Chipping Norton by bus each day and closing the cosy little building by the church in the centre of the village. The party was an annual affair; her mother had always been one of its organisers and Katrina had taken over this task. She had already planned the tea and been to a meeting about presents for the children, but the tree would need new baubles. She said: 'O.K., give me ten minutes. Have you sent your cards yet?'

They left the room and started downstairs. 'Mrs Beale's doing the envelopes today,' Lucius told her.

Mrs Beale was an elderly treasure who arrived twice a week to deal with any correspondence Lucius hadn't time for. She saw to the wages sheets too and sat in on the weekly sessions he had with the Home Farm Manager. Katrina nodded. 'What a paragon she is—what are you giving her for Christmas? I found a rather nice scarf in Liberty's.'

'You shall help me choose something.' He went on down the staircase and left her to run to her room and change into a skirt and cashmere woolly and matching top coat, cram her feet into boots, stuff her shoulder bag with necessary odds and ends, and then go to the kitchen. Lucius was in the hall and as she went past him she asked: 'Do you want to eat here this evening?'

He didn't answer at once, then: 'That would have been nice, but I've a date.'

She barely paused on her way. 'O.K. Blonde and beautiful, I suppose.' She said it lightly and felt surprised at her disappointment; she was a bit lonely without Virginia around the house, of course, but no one needed to know that.

She asked Mrs Beecham to let her have a tray in the sitting room when she got back that evening. 'I'm sure to have an enormous lunch, so soup and an omelette will be fine,' she said.

Mrs Beecham gave her a thoughtful glance. 'I hope you both have a nice day,' she observed. 'It's a pity Mr Massey can't come back for dinner; there's the tenderest capon in the larder.'

'Another time, Mrs Beecham!' Katrina nipped away before Mrs Beecham had time to frame the next question. 'I'll be back about six o'clock,' she told Lovelace.

'Probably nearer seven,' said Lucius as he ushered her through the door.

The Jaguar wasn't there. Katrina stood gazing open-mouthed. 'That's a Bentley Turbo,' she said at last.

'Yes—I drove it back yesterday. I'll be needing a second car.' He didn't tell her why, and she didn't ask. She thought she knew; when all this silly nonsense Virginia had started was over and done with he would get married. Perhaps it was the girl he had the date with that evening; he would, she thought shrewdly, have to use all his considerable charm to convince her that going on holiday to Greece with a girl he had practically grown up with was absolutely nothing to worry about. She had no doubt that he would succeed.

'She's super,' she observed. 'Is she easy to drive?'

'Goes like a bird. Get in and I'll show you.'

It was indeed a magnificent car, and Katrina was sorry when Lucius parked in the mews behind his office, told her to stay where she was for five minutes and disappeared inside.

'We'll leave her here,' he said when he got back, 'and get a taxi. Where shall it be first? Shall we try Fortnum and Mason for the crackers and something for Mrs Beale, have lunch and take a look at some holiday clothes for you?'

She was getting out of the car. 'All right, Lucius. You're sure you want me to come with you? I mean, it wouldn't really matter if I didn't, would it?'

He looked down at her, frowning, his grey eyes cool. 'Backing out?' he wanted to know. 'You never used to, Katie.'

That stung. 'Well, I'm not. I just wanted to make sure.' She reflected rather sadly that until now she would have asked him to tell her who the girl was, even offered advice about marrying her, just as a sister might, but somehow she couldn't. She hadn't felt shy or awkward with Lucius in the whole of her life, but now she did, and she didn't like it.

They had a wonderful time choosing the crackers, first for the children's party, then for themselves, and while they were there it seemed a pity not to buy some of the delicacies so temptingly on display. Julius arranged for their

purchases to be sent round to his office, hailed a
taxi and bore her off to lunch; Claridges, as he had
promised.

From there, fortified by hot lobster patties,
roast turkey and a soufflé Harlequin, washed
down by hock, they made their way to the
boutique where Katrina had bought her dresses.
She was welcomed as an old customer, Lucius was
settled at a discreet distance, and the saleslady and
her assistants, warmly enthusiastic at the idea of a
holiday in Greece, brought out armfuls of
colourful garments.

'Oh, I wouldn't want half of those,' declared
Katrina, and then, quite carried away, bought
almost all of them—tops and skirts, Italian
knitteds, vivid scarves, slacks. They totalled an
astronomical figure, and she wrote the cheque with
a steady hand before rejoining Lucius.

The packages would be parcelled up and ready
within half an hour, she was assured, as she
floated out of the shop, quite carried away with
her extravagance. On the pavement outside she
recovered sufficiently to say: 'We still have to buy
something for Mrs Beale.'

Lucius smiled faintly. 'So we do. What do you
suggest?'

'One of those big square shawls—paisley and
fringed; she could use it if she goes out in the
evening, or just when she's at home—I mean, she
wouldn't have to put it away in a drawer, if you
see what I mean.'

He agreed seriously enough and then asked:
'You seem to have bought a great deal, Katie.'

'I've been wickedly extravagant, but everything
was so bright and pretty.' She added anxiously: 'I
shall never have the chance to wear them all, shall I?'

'Undoubtedly. I can't wait to see you in them.'

She remembered then that he had a date that evening. 'We ought to be getting back,' she said firmly, and refused the tea he offered her, saying she had a great deal to do when she got home. It vexed her rather that he didn't try to persuade her to do anything else.

He dropped her off outside her front door with the excuse that he was already a little late, so she said quite sharply: 'I'll get Lovelace to help with the parcels—don't get out.' It annoyed her very much that he took her at her word.

She didn't see him for the next two days; indeed, it wasn't until the afternoon of the third day, when she was knee deep in children playing Hunt the Slipper, serving jellies and ice creams and handing out balloons, that he appeared, armed with a great tin of sweets which he handed out by the fistful. He was popular with the children, even though they were in slight awe of him, and he sat down at the long trestle table and ate a jelly with an unselfconscious pleasure which she found endearing.

The party ended with the pulling of crackers and handing out of a present to each child, and the various ladies who had come to help started on the clearing up, while the school caretaker, a cantankerous old man, began to dismantle the tables and chairs. Lucius filled the car with children who lived outside the village and drove off with them. The school was itself once again by the time he got back and Katrina was getting into her own car. He got out of his car and put his head through the window, within inches of her face. 'Go and wash your sticky fingers,' he told her. 'I'll call for you in half an hour.'

'But Mrs Beecham will have started cooking dinner,' she protested.

'Then she can eat it. You're having dinner with me. I've got all my presents to wrap and I need some help.' She sighed loudly. 'You're so helpless!'

'Yes, I know, that's why I want some help.' He smiled gently at her and she said: 'All right—half an hour, then.'

Actually the evening was fun. They ate their dinner in the little morning room at a small round table before a roaring fire and then went into the drawing room where the presents had been piled high on one of the sofas. Katrina wrapped each carefully, examining it first, while Lucius tied on the labels. One or two of the boxes she wasn't allowed to open and she amused herself guessing what was inside.

'Wait and see,' said Lucius. 'What have you got for Virginia and James?'

'Table linen for their patio—white linen appliquéd with flowers. Mrs Lovell said they always had lunch there in the summer, so I daresay Virginia will do the same.' She added: 'I've not heard from them.'

'Did you expect to? They're spending Christmas in the Bahamas, aren't they? I'd rather be here.'

'Oh, so would I.' Katrina looked around her at the grand room, somehow so homelike and cosy with the three dogs bunched before the fire and Lucius sprawled out in his chair. 'I think Bouncer considers this place his home.'

Lucius glanced up. 'Possibly. How strange it will be when we don't visit each other any more.'

She looked bewildered and then said quickly: 'Yes, won't it?' She hadn't quite understood; she would think it over, later, she couldn't dismiss it as a chance remark because Lucius never made chance remarks. To get away from her unease she asked: 'Which date do we leave for Greece?'

'January the tenth, that gives us time to breathe after the New Year.'

'Virginia and James don't get back until the fifteenth . . .'

'That's why we're going on the tenth. You're going to Lady Ryder's tomorrow evening? I'll pick you up and you can invite me to dinner afterwards.'

'All right. I'll get Mrs Beecham to make one of those mince tarts you like so much.' She glanced at the lovely old bracket clock on its ledge between the windows. 'Heavens, look at the time. I must go home.'

It had been a pleasant day she told herself sleepily, lying curled up in her bed later, and she had enjoyed it, doing the parcels with Lucius. He was a pleasant person to be with; true, he had a nasty temper, but he seldom allowed it to show and just lately he had been positively mild. Possibly because he'd got his own way with this silly business of pretending to fancy her. It was kind of him, of course. Perhaps he had thought that she would mind people gossiping about Virginia's silly remarks; he had said so, hadn't he? She shut her eyes tightly and frowned. Tomorrow she would ask him about the girl he'd dated. Perhaps after all this time, he had really fallen in love—properly in love—at last. She found the thought upsetting, but she was too tired to bother; she fell asleep and dreamed that she was bridesmaid at his wedding—the bride was tantalisingly out of focus, but Lucius wore the look of a man who had got his own way and was delighted with himself. To her great surprise she woke up crying.

CHAPTER FIVE

LADY Ryder's parties were a class apart. She lived in a small Queen Anne house in the centre of the village, looked after by a grumpy middle-aged housekeeper and an equally grumpy old man who saw to the small but delightful garden, drove her around in an elderly Austin motor car, and opened the front door to callers. Twice a year she invited her friends to her house, where she crammed in as many people as possible, serving them with indifferent sherry, very small meat-paste sandwiches and sweet biscuits. And everyone came because it was an open secret that she had almost no money now that she was widowed and even such refreshments as she offered were a drain on her slender purse. And in return she was invited everywhere; seldom a week went past without her dining out, enjoying drinks with some friend or other, or being bidden to tea. She was an imposing old lady, very upright, with beady eyes and a hawk's nose and a resounding voice, much given to criticism but never known to utter a single complaint about her circumstances. Everyone loved her; although when she had been extra tart, with reservations.

The low-ceilinged drawing room was already full by the time Katrina and Lucius arrived. They found their hostess, accepted sherry from the old man and circulated, which meant edging their way gingerly from group to group and shouting greetings above the din. It wasn't long before they were separated, and Katrina found herself with Mrs Turner, Mrs Lovell and two youngish women she didn't know.

'My nieces,' observed Mrs Lovell, 'Madeleine and Sylvia—spending a few days with me. You must come over and have a chat while they're here.'

The women smiled sweetly and eyed Katrina's velvet suit with calculating stares. She decided she didn't like them and said at once: 'I'm up to my eyes, Mrs Lovell, getting ready for Christmas. Have you heard from Virginia and James?'

Mrs Lovell shook her head. 'I thought I might give a party for them when they get back—you'll come, of course. Do you suppose Lucius would come too, or would he feel embarrassed?'

Katrina tried to remember if she had ever known him embarrassed, and decided that she hadn't, but before she could answer one of the girls asked eagerly: 'Why would he be that, Aunt?'

Mrs Lovell, seldom the centre of attention, saw her chance; at some length she embarked on an account of Virginia's close friendship with Lucius. 'We quite thought that they would marry,' she ended, 'but it wasn't Virginia at all, but Katrina.'

Two pairs of hard eyes studied her with ill-concealed astonishment before focusing on Lucius, standing at the far end of the room. His size and height alone made him stand out in a crowd. His good looks and his elegance were an added bonus; he could have walked off with any one of the pretty young women in the room. Madeleine and Sylvia returned their gaze to Katrina once more, their astonishment more eloquent than words. She gave the pair of them a limpid look, murmured,

'So nice to have met you. Excuse me—there's someone I simply have to speak to . . .' and slid away to join the Frobishers.

She had barely returned their greetings when she found Lucius beside her. He bent to whisper in her ear: 'You're decidedly ruffled—is it the sherry?'

She shook her head, smiling a little. He flung an arm round her shoulders and talked nonsense to the Frobisher girls, who loved it, but presently he said: 'Katie, Lady Ryder wants to talk to you,' and eased her away, with perfect manners, to make their way across the room to where the old lady was sitting.

'There you are,' she declared loudly. 'Our future bride—why aren't you wearing a ring?'

There was a sudden pause in the talk around them, resumed almost at once, and Lucius bent down and whispered something in her ear. Whatever it was sent her off into peals of laughter, caused all those nearby to look frustrated and sent a nice pink flush to Katrina's cheeks.

All the same she answered civilly when Lady Ryder made some remark about her dress, and even contrived a smile, carefully avoiding Lucius's eye. She wished with all her heart she could box his ears for him.

She didn't allow her feelings to show, however, and it wasn't until they were driving back that she said coldly: 'You behaved abominably—letting everyone see . . . I can find no possible excuse for you . . .'

'You said that before, dear girl. Don't you want to know what I said to Lady Ryder?'

'No, I don't,' snapped Katrina, and spoilt it immediately by adding: 'What did you say?'

'Women!' observed Lucius to no one in particular, and didn't tell her.

'I refuse to quarrel about such a trifling thing,' declared Katrina huffily as he drew up before her door.

He turned in his seat and kissed her swiftly. 'That's a good girl,' he said kindly, and got out of the car.

They ate Mrs Beecham's excellent dinner unhurriedly and on perfectly good terms with each other; there was a great deal to talk about. Christmas loomed large now; its advent touched off a round of mild gaieties to follow Lady Ryder's party—carol singers, decorating the tree in the church, and just who Katrina should invite for drinks on Christmas Eve.

'How many have you got coming?' she wanted to know. 'There'll be your cousin Dora, I suppose, and Bertie and the two boys, and Great-Uncle Tom and little Tom and Jeremy, and Aunt Lucy . . .'

'You remember better than I do—Jeremy's bringing his fiancée and Aunt Lucy's got a companion.'

Katrina counted on her fingers. 'That's eleven with you—there'll be about thirty of us. Drinks about half past six.'

'And you will come back to my place for dinner. I'll pick you up for church on Christmas morning and take you back with me to Stockley.'

'Yes, but that means I'll be with you all day,' she objected.

He smiled at her across the table. 'That's the idea, Katie.'

She wasn't quite sure what he meant by that. 'Are we dressing up in the evening?'

'Oh, lord, yes. Wear the pink dress. No one will do much on Boxing Day; we could ride before breakfast.'

Katrina agreed cheerfully. She had been secretly dreading Christmas, but Lucius had it all planned out and although his family weren't exactly exciting, he was a good host and saw to it that everyone enjoyed themselves. They parted presently, still on friendly terms. Katrina had forgotten that she hadn't enjoyed Lady Ryder's party overmuch. She went to bed, her head full of plans for the party on Christmas Eve.

The days before Christmas flew by. Lucius went up to London and she didn't see him for several days and when he returned he offered no explanation. Not that she expected one and she wouldn't have dreamed of asking. They rode together, spent an afternoon helping to decorate the tree in the church and compared notes about the carol singers. They had each received visits from several groups by now; very small children who sang the opening bars of 'The First Noel', and then beat a tattoo on the door knocker, to be refreshed with hot cocoa and biscuits, and the weighty members of the church choir, reinforced by an outer fringe of men from the village, who sang at least two carols before knocking, far more gently than the children, and who were admitted to the hall, to drink beer and eat hot mince pies. They made their rounds to a regular pattern, beginning with the smaller houses in the village, working their way round the doctor's house, the vicarage, the handful of houses occupied by retired people, then Katrina's home, and last, Stockley House, where Lucius, being lord of the manor, handed out glasses of port, hot coffee and sausage rolls, as well as a discreet envelope towards the choir outing.

Two days before Christmas Eve, coming back

from an early morning ride, Lucius asked: 'What are you going to wear for your party?'

Katrina looked surprised. It wasn't like Lucius to bother about her clothes, and this was the third time in as many weeks. She took a mental survey of her wardrobe and said: 'Well, there's that patterned blue velvet I had last year . . .'

'We'll go to town tomorrow and find something.'

She turned to look at him. 'Look, Lucius—I've got plenty of clothes. What's got into you? I hadn't planned to buy any more for ages.'

'All the more reason to do so. I'll call for you about half past nine.'

They went in the Bentley and parked at his office as they had done before, had coffee and went in search of a dress. They found it very shortly, laid enticingly across a small gilt chair, sharing the elegant little window with a bowl of Christmas roses and an artfully arranged chiffon scarf. 'That's it,' declared Lucius. 'You go and buy it while I pop into that phone box and book a table for lunch.'

The dress fitted. It also looked extremely nice on her. The price was ridiculously high, but Katrina signed a cheque with only a passing thought of the hole it was going to make in her bank balance, reflecting at the same time that Lucius was taking an unwonted interest in her clothes lately. Meant kindly, she supposed, an attempt by an old friend to smarten up her image. She left the shop, found him waiting patiently, handed him the bandbox, and remarked that she was hungry.

'The girl I took out to lunch the other day would only eat quails' eggs and Melba toast,' Lucius told her.

'Was she ill?' asked Katrina seriously.

'Not to my knowledge. She held strong views about female curves getting too curvy, which prevented her from eating like us common mortals who aren't bothered about a few extra pounds.'

'You speak for yourself! Although I don't think I could bear to eat quails' eggs and Melba toast.' She cast him a suspicious look. 'What are you laughing about? Am I getting fat?'

'Not a bit of it—just right, Katie.' He hailed a taxi. 'I've got a table at the Mirabelle.'

As they got into the taxi, she asked: 'Is that where you got the quails' eggs?'

'Don't fish, my dear, or should I be flattered that you're at last taking an interest in my life style?'

'Oh, pooh,' said Katrina, just a little too quickly. It astonished her to discover that until just lately she hadn't bothered her head much about Lucius's life, yet now, suddenly, she felt a lively interest in it.

They lunched deliciously, finishing with fresh peaches in champagne, and then they made their way back to the car, stopping to look in shop windows as they went. There was an early dusk creeping through the streets as Lucius started on the slow business of getting out of London, but once they were free of the last suburbs, he tore smoothly along the motorway until he was forced to slow at Oxford.

'This is a very nice car,' said Katrina happily. 'Is it fun to drive?'

'Yes, but don't think you're going to borrow it, because you're not.'

'I might save up and buy one.'

He said, suddenly serious: 'Don't, Katie. She'd

be a bit much for you—you're a very good driver, but I'd not have a moment's peace.'

'You mean I might smash the car up? Well, I won't buy one, then, only perhaps you might let me drive this one, just once with you here, of course.' Her quiet voice was gently wheedling.

He said at once: 'Of course. We'll take her for a run tomorrow afternoon.'

'I've got to go over to Mrs Lovell's—I couldn't get out of going to tea. I don't want to; I've far too much to do at home. I've got to talk to Mrs Beecham about their Christmas dinner and talk to Lovelace . . .'

'Proper little housewife, aren't you, my dear? We'll drive over to the Lovells' place and she can give me a cup of tea and you shall drive back.'

Mrs Lovell was delighted to see him, and so were her nieces. He was charming to them both, charming to Mrs Lovell, and nonetheless managed to convey that Katrina was the centre of his world. She squirmed under his air of loving proprietorship, the smiling glances and frequent darlings. On the way back driving the Bentley with determined sangfroid she said stonily: 'You overdid it, Lucius. I felt like a mid-Victorian Miss with no rights of her own.'

He said imperturbably: 'Change gear, Katie. You aren't exactly one of the stalwarts of Women's Lib.—besides, I wanted to leave a good impression.'

She gasped and took a corner too fast. 'What of?' she demanded.

'Devotion to you'.

'Oh, stuff,' said Katrina, and missed a slow moving farm tractor by a hair's breadth.

Lucius remained calm. 'If you bust her up it will

cost you fifty-six thousand pounds,' he told her. 'I shall dock it off your dress allowance.'

She drove carefully after that, not speaking. Only when they drew up at her home did she say in a rather high voice: 'Thank you for letting me drive. She's a lovely car.' She opened her door. 'Goodnight, Lucius.'

He was already out though, walking to the door opened by Lovelace and going through it with all the assurance of a welcome guest.

'I could do with a drink,' he suggested, 'my nerves have been shaken.'

'Oh, rubbish,' said Katrina crossly, 'you haven't a nerve in your body. You'll find the whisky in the usual place; I'll be with you in a minute.'

When she went back to the sitting room he was sitting in the winged armchair before the fire, the whisky on the table at his elbow. He got up as she went in and crossed to the sofa table where the drinks were.

'Madeira?' he suggested. 'Something to put a little stiffening into you.'

She bristled. 'Stiffening? Are you suggesting that I drove badly?'

'You drove very well indeed.' He handed her the drink and after she had settled herself by the fire sat down too.

'Have you any indigent aunts or cousins?' he asked her.

She choked on her wine. 'One or two, yes. Why on earth do you ask?'

Lucius gave her a look of such blandness that she sat up, prepared to hear something outrageous.

'Well, you will live with me, naturally, but it would be nice to keep this place in the family, wouldn't it? The eldest son couldn't have it, of course, he'd inherit Stockley, but the second son might find it very useful.'

She choked so hard this time that he had to get up and pat her on the back. When she had her breath: 'I so wish you wouldn't talk such nonsense!'

'It's as well to get these things sorted out now. Parents shouldn't argue in front of the children.'

She swallowed the rest of her Madeira. 'What are you talking about? Whose children, and who's going to argue?'

'Ours,' he said calmly, 'and us. Which reminds me, it's about time you had this.' He put his hand in a pocket and took out a small leather case and opened it. 'We have that quaint old custom of handing on the engagement ring . . .'

It was a very beautiful sapphire, set in a circle of diamonds and mounted in an old-fashioned gold setting. Katrina goggled at it as he took her hand and slipped the ring on to the third finger. 'I daresay you remember my mother wearing it,' he observed. 'Why do you look so surprised?' He bent and kissed her cheek. 'Have you quite forgotten that I'm bowled over by your elegance and brains, worldliness and maturity? A girl with all those assets at her fingertips shouldn't look like a stunned fish.'

Katrina stared up at him and then back to the ring. For some reason she couldn't fathom she badly wanted to burst into tears. She said in a quiet little voice: 'No, I hadn't forgotten. It's a very beautiful ring.' She added after a moment: 'Thank you, Lucius.' She looked at the ring. 'Only it's under false pretences, isn't it?'

He bent and kissed her, an impersonal,

brotherly salute on her cheek. 'Dear girl', was all he said, and then: 'Since I'm here you might as well ask me to dinner.'

It was the least she could do, she supposed; she asked Lovelace to lay and warn Mrs Beecham, and was very conscious of his elderly eyes on the ring.

Lucius didn't stay late. With a cheerful: 'What time are we coming tomorrow evening?' he took himself off. His various relatives would be arriving in the morning and he was in for a busy time of it, his goodnight was casual in the extreme, although he did thank her for his dinner. For some time after he had gone, Katrina sat there by the fire, watching the sapphire glow in its light. It was ridiculous that she should feel sad and unhappy. Christmas, with all its attendant pleasures, was only a little more than a day away, she had nothing to be miserable about. Virginia was happily married, she had a lovely home, old, faithful servants, plenty of friends, enough money . . . Any moment now she would burst into tears. She got briskly to her feet and took herself off to bed.

There was no time to feel miserable the next day; there was far too much to do. Old John had brought down his prized chrysanthemums, bundles of holly and mistletoe and the bowls of paper whites he had been forcing, and Katrina busied herself arranging these around the house, before going down to the stables to saddle Gem. It was a cold grey day, and she only rode for an hour, leaving Gem to be rubbed down by the boy from the village and going back to the house to shower and change and spend what time there was before lunch in the studio. This time the drawings were better; she felt reasonably content before she went downstairs to Mrs Beecham's soup and omelette. As soon as Christmas was over, she promised herself she would get down to her work; a day or two would be enough.

She went along to the kitchen presently to see if Mrs Beecham needed any help, but beyond setting out canapés on china plates and eating the cheese tartlets almost as fast as Mrs Beecham could get them out of the oven, there was little for her to do. Christmas dinner was already organised; there would be turkey and Christmas pudding and everything which went with them, and Katrina had told Lovelace to fetch up a couple of bottles of hock from the cellar. She had provided beer as well, because Old John didn't hold with wine drinking. There would be quite a cheerful party in the kitchen, as the girls who came up from the village each day would join Mrs Beecham and Lovelace, as well as the boy who helped in the stables and Old John. She made sure that they would lack nothing, sneaked another tartlet, and went back to the sitting room.

Lovelace had readied the drawing room for the evening. It looked warm and welcoming with the table lamps already on to keep out the early dusk and a good fire burning. Katrina turned her back on it reluctantly and took Bouncer for a walk. From the top of the hill she could see Stockley looming in the last of the afternoon's light. There were several cars parked on the sweep and lights shone from a number of windows in the great house. She stood looking at it and felt lonely.

She turned and went home, Bouncer racing to and fro, delighted with himself. The old house welcomed them as they went in, Bouncer to sink happily on to the rug before the fire in the sitting room and Katrina to take off her outdoor things and join him in the chair. They shared their tea and then she went upstairs to change into her dress.

Lucius had been right, she had to admit; the sapphire blue suited her. She inspected herself carefully and as she was turning away from the mirror remembered the ring. She would have to wear it—not in private, though; it was all part and parcel of Lucius's outrageous plan and she wore it because he expected her to, but only when there were other people around. She went downstairs and met Lovelace in the hall. His eye looked for the ring and found it, although he said nothing, but he smiled at her in a fatherly fashion, just as he had always done when she had been a little girl and shown him birthday presents, or school prizes, and she found herself smiling back at him. 'I'm going to have a sherry before they all arrive, Lovelace,' she told him, and went into the drawing room.

They came in a thin trickle to start with and then everyone at once, and at the very end, Lucius ushered his party in. Katrina knew them all, and went from one to the other, laughing and talking until she found herself quiet for a moment and Lucius beside her. He took her hand and looked down at it and smiled.

'That's a very becoming dress,' he told her, 'and how well it goes with the ring.' He took two glasses from the tray Lovelace was carrying. 'I'm going to tell everyone here that we're engaged.' He added: 'With your permission, of course.'

Which he didn't wait for. He made the announcement quietly in his calm deep voice, still holding her hand, and the moment he started to speak the chatter died down, just as though everyone there had been expecting him to tell them something momentous. The minute that he had finished they all crowded round, congratulating, drinking healths, kissing and shaking hands. And the women all wanted to see the ring, of course. Katrina, caught off balance, smiled and murmured and smiled again, her hand held fast in Lucius's firm grip. It was like being in a dream; she seemed to have lost all power to think sensibly; it couldn't be happening to her—until now Lucius's preposterous idea, brought to light from time to time, had still been vague enough for her to ignore it for most of the time, and even when she had thought about it, she supposed she had never quite believed it. All the same, he could have warned her. She was as surprised as her guests, probably more so.

The news lengthened the party considerably, and it was well after eight o'clock by the time the last guest had gone home. She had had no chance to speak to Lucius and now, as Lovelace shut the door finally, Lucius said: 'Run and get your coat, Katie. The others will be famished if we don't join them at once. I bought some champagne for your people; you don't mind if I let them have it now?'

She shook her head; he seemed to have thought of everything. When she had had time to pull herself together she thought peevishly, running up the stairs to her room, she would call a halt to his nonsense. She got back in time to see a delighted Lovelace accepting several bottles of champagne. His elderly face creased into a smile as he saw her.

'I'm sure we're delighted, Miss Katrina—what a splendid piece of news, if I may say so! How pleased Mr and Mrs Gibson would have been—the families being so close, as it were, and you and Mr Lucius being so close too.'

He went on his dignified way to the kitchen, and Katrina said: 'I should go to the kitchen with him and tell Mrs Beecham.'

Lucius opened the door. 'I told Lovelace that we'd both go when I bring you back after dinner.'

She said quietly: 'Aren't you taking a lot for granted, Lucius? I'm not a child to be ordered about, you know.'

He said gently: 'You always left everything to me when you were a little girl—you trusted me then, I wish you would trust me now.'

She shivered a little in the cold air seeping in through the open door. She said sharply: 'I'm not a little girl, I'm twenty-seven. And I don't understand why you're doing this—I can't believe it's just to get even with Virginia. You said it was to make things easier for me here, and I suppose that's true. Only I feel a fraud . . .'

'No need.' He took her arm and went into the night, shutting the door behind them, settling her in the car and getting in beside her. 'But you still trust me?'

'I can't ever remember you letting me down. Yes, I trust you, Lucius.' She added: 'But I don't see why you're going to such lengths.'

Lucius said harshly: 'I don't want even the gentlest snigger made at your expense, not even a small smile from your dearest friends. Virginia may not have meant to do harm, to hold you up to ridicule, get cheap laughs at your expense, but she could have succeeded. You're liked—loved—by everyone who knows you, my dear, but we all have our human failings, and one is to enjoy another's discomfiture even while one is sympathizing.'

He started the car and they had made the short journey to his house before she answered. 'I feel so ashamed—that I ever thought you were just getting the better of Virginia—to teach her a lesson.' She turned to look at him. 'Lucius, I think you must be the best friend anyone could wish for.'

He didn't answer, only dropped a casual kiss on the top of her head.

Hours later, curled up in her bed, sleepily going over the evening, she concluded that it was one of the nicest of the year. Lucius's family had been charming to her, they had toasted the pair of them in champagne, welcomed her warmly as a member of the family and urged a wedding as soon as possible. They had dined then, Lucius's traditional Christmas Eve dinner: lobster soup, eggs en cocotte à la crème, roast sirloin of beef and horseradish, and a superb trifle by way of pudding. There had been Muscadet and claret, and brandy with the coffee, although she hadn't had that; she hadn't needed it either. She had been happy enough, feeeling relaxed for the first time in weeks.

She was up early the next morning. Other Christmases, when Virginia had been at home, they had opened their presents together after breakfast, but the idea of sitting alone doing this didn't bear thinking of. Lovelace and Mrs Beecham and Maudie and Annie, the second girl from the village, were going to join her in the sitting room and bring Old John and the boy with them. They came in ushered by Lovelace, chorused 'A Merry Christmas' to her, received their gifts, handed her a large square package and stood waiting while she opened it—a wooden fruit bowl, simple, well polished and eminently usable. 'So you can take it with you when you go to Stockley

House, Miss Katrina,' explained Mrs Beecham, 'and if only we'd known in time, we'd have got a little something for Mr Lucius. And we did appreciate him coming with you to the kitchens last night to tell us you're going to be married. Having known you both for such a long time, me and Lovelace were fair honoured, as you might say.'

'It's beautiful, and I—we shall use it constantly. Thank you all very much. I haven't had time to talk to you, but you'll all stay on here, of course, if—when I go. We thought we might ask someone in the family to come and live here.'

Lovelace gave a dignified nod. 'A very suitable idea, Miss Katrina. I presume the house will stay in the family for future use?'

'Yes, that's right, Lovelace. But we'll talk about that later—it won't be just yet. Mr Lucius and I are going on holiday after the New Year.'

'So we've been given to understand, Miss Katrina. Will you have coffee before you leave for church?'

'No, thank you—or just a moment. Mr Lucius will be fetching me, if he's early we might even have a cup together.'

When they'd gone, Katrina turned to her own pile of gifts stacked neatly on the sofa table—any number of them. Like a child she opened the ones from friends first, putting the labels carefully on one side, admiring the handkerchiefs, the bottles of scent, the notepaper and boxes of soap; and then turning to the family presents; aunts and uncles she seldom saw but who exchanged a gift with her each Christmas. They had all done her proud this year—delicate figurines of porcelain, a charming vase, a silver photo frame, and the

Massey family had, as they always did, clubbed together. This year it was a glass scent bottle with a delicate opaque flower stopper. There was nothing from Virginia and James, but she excused them instantly; they had been far too busy with their wedding preparations to have had time for Christmas presents. There were three packages left now, and she undid the first one with a glance at the clock. She would have to get ready for church. Lucius would be here in ten minutes or so.

She was staring at the contents as the door opened and he came in.

'Merry Christmas,' he said cheerfully, and took the diamond and sapphire brooch from her and pinned it on to her dress.

'Lucius, it's gorgeous! Thank you very much, and a Happy Christmas.' She lifted her face as unselfconsciously as a child and he kissed her cheek. 'Do you want coffee? Is there time?'

He went over to the brass wall bell and tugged it. 'Ten minutes or more. They'll wait for us anyway.' He said it without arrogance, accepting it as his right as lord of the manor. 'Open the other two while the coffee comes.'

An antique pearl-studded heart on a gold chain, thin as a spider's thread, and in the third and last box a pearl studded gold bangle. Katrina put them both on and went to study herself in the great mirror hanging on the wall. 'But Lucius,' she protested hesitantly, 'three things—I mean, the brooch is beautiful . . . You're too generous!'

Lovelace came in with the coffee tray and he poured them each a cup. 'I like giving you presents,' he said quietly, 'and I'm glad you like them.'

'Oh, I do, I do, only I don't feel I deserve

them. I'm not even beautiful enough to do them justice.'

He smiled. 'You've got that round the wrong way, my dear. Drink your coffee and pop on a hat and coat.'

The little church was crowded, and since the Massey pews were at the front, they had to walk the length of the aisle. Katrina was very conscious of the smiling stares and more than thankful to have Lucius's calm bulk beside her. The family pews were full, of course; the younger cousins had overflowed into the pew behind, but two places had been kept for Lucius and herself. Her own pew was empty. Singing the opening carol while the choir, in clean surplices, processed to their places, she thought busily. Hardly the place in which to arrange one's future, she reminded herself, but she didn't seem able to stop herself. She would have to persuade one of her elderly aunts to come and live in her home. She drew a breath. Here she was making plans, just as though she and Lucius were going to get married even though he had said that after a time they would let their engagement peter out ... she wondered how you petered out an engagement without loss of dignity. Were they to come back from Greece disengaged again? And wouldn't that cause people to gossip even more than they had done over Virginia's wild statements?

She frowned and sighed, unaware that Lucius's eyes were upon her face, reading every thought there.

On their way back in the car, he said: 'You didn't hear a word of Mr Moffat's excellent sermon and half the time you forgot to sing. What's troubling you, Katie?'

There wasn't time to tell him. She said brightly that there was absolutely nothing the matter and began to talk about the day ahead of them, wishing with all her heart that she was one of those clever women who always knew what they were doing and why, and had an answer for every problem—perhaps they were clever enough not to have problems.

The day unfolded itself into the pattern of countless former Christmas days—drinks, while everyone thanked everyone else for their presents, a buffet lunch of delicious bits and pieces, a walk through the park for those who wanted while the elderlies dozed, and then tea round the fire in the drawing room; muffins in old-fashioned muffin dishes, paper-thin china, tiny sandwiches and the Christmas cake. It was a leisurely meal with everyone talking at once and a lot of laughter, and Katrina, sitting on the floor beside the oldest Uncle Massey's chair, was content.

Presently Lucius drove her back home to change for the evening. Dinner on Christmas night was something of an event at Stockley, and everyone was dressed accordingly. She had decided on the new pink dress, a happy foil for her new jewellery, but first she went along to the kitchens to see how Lovelace and his companions were enjoying their day. Splendidly, they assured her, while she approved of the table decked ready for their own meal.

'Everyone's coming for tea tomorrow, Mrs Beecham—could you cope? All the Massey family—that's eleven—and me. I shall be at Stockley for lunch and dinner. We're riding before breakfast and I expect Mr Lucius will have it with me here. Could you manage that?

And scones for tea—Great-Uncle Tom loves them.'

'You just leave it to me, Miss Katrina,' Mrs Beecham beamed across the table, 'and I'll pop one of my chocolate sponges in the oven with them.'

Katrina bathed and dressed slowly. There was time enough and she wanted to look her best. The rose-coloured silk was certainly delightful and gave her rather mousy looks a glow. She took pains with her hair and face, collected a purse and slippers, picked up her coat and went downstairs to wait for Lucius.

He was there in the sitting room when she went in, leaning his weight against the drum table between the windows, reading a letter. He looked up as she went in, put the letter into a pocket and went to meet her.

'You're early', she observed matter-of-factly.

'I needed a few minutes' peace and quiet.' He studied her slowly. 'That's charming', he told her. 'You know, Katie, given the right clothes, you'd be a pretty girl.'

This from Lucius was praise indeed; she thanked him warmly and added: 'You chose the dress.'

He took her hands and stood smiling down at her. 'I've chosen the girl too.'

She smiled, with the unspoken thought that it was only a temporary choice, after all. She dismissed it at once because it made her sad, and Christmas Day wasn't meant for sadness; which meant that she took care to be a good deal more animated than she usually was, chattering away in a most untypical manner as he drove her back to Stockley House.

The vast hall was quiet as they went inside.

Cobb took her coat before Lucius waved him away, his footsteps hardly sounded on the thick carpet, just as the voices in the drawing room were muffled by old walls and heavy drapes. She had started to cross the hall, but Lucius stopped her with a hand on her arm.

'There's something . . .' he began. 'What's on your mind, Katie? I thought we had everything settled, but you look as though you're on the verge of making some great discovery.' He smiled at her as he spoke, but she didn't smile back; she was tonguetied, frozen into immobility, because that was exactly what she had just done. Made a great discovery—that she was in love with Lucius, standing there so bland and calm—like a brother, she thought furiously. She longed to shake that calm even while she admitted that she had no idea how to set about it.

CHAPTER SIX

SHE thought of their conversation in the hall
before they left. Katrina had found her voice;
rather high and wooden, but still a voice. She said
inanely: 'Oh, yes—really? Well...' and then:
'Would you like a drink?'

Lucius was looking at her very intently, his grey
eyes thoughtful. 'No, thanks. There's punch
waiting for us, Great-Uncle Tom's own recipe,
heaven help us all.' He smiled then and she had
smiled back at him carefully. On no account must
he ever discover her feelings about him; she must
remember to be the old friend, the girl from next
door. Providentially Lovelace came into the room,
and she turned away from Lucius to ask him if
they had all they needed in the kitchen and to
wish him goodnight. 'Don't wait up, Lovelace,'
she told him. 'I shan't be late, but I'll lock up as I
come in.'

Lovelace preceded them into the hall and
opened the door. 'Very well, Miss Katrina. We all
hope you both enjoy a good evening.'

The echo of their combined thanks hung on the
frosty air as they got into the car.

'We're riding in the morning?' asked Lucius as
he started the car.

To refuse would make him ask why. 'Yes, I'd
like to. Would you like to come back to breakfast?'

'Thanks. What are you doing for the rest of the
day?' He added slowly: 'We ought to spend it
together, you know.'

Katrina said in what she hoped was a perfectly natural voice: 'Oh dear—and I promised I'd go over to Mrs Lovell's.' Which was quite true in a way, she had, but she hadn't said when. 'Lunch,' she added; she would have to take the car somewhere, have lunch at a pub, and stay away until teatime.

'Dinner, then,' said Lucius, and this time she had agreed meekly.

Christmas dinner was as traditional as Christmas Eve's had been: lobster patties, roast turkey with a vast assortment of vegetables, little sausages, and a huge baked ham, and then the pudding, aflame with brandy and borne to the table with ceremony by Cobb. There were trifles, jellies, fresh fruit salad, thick rich cream and brandy butter, and lastly Welsh rarebit and Stilton with the port. The meal took a long time because everyone talked so much, but finally at Dora's signal, Katrina, Jeremy's fiancée, and Miss Porter, the companion, rose from the table and went back to the drawing room, where naturally enough and not at all to Katrina's liking, the talk was of weddings; hers and Lucius's in particular, of course. She reminded herself that they were all kindly disposed towards her, their eager talk of white satin, bridesmaids and whether to have the full choir was genuinely friendly, and it seemed to her to be positively unkind to contradict them in any way. She murmured in what she hoped was a noncommittal way and was relieved when the men joined them, but only briefly, for Lucius made no effort to divert the talk into other channels—indeed, he positively encouraged his guests to wallow in a lengthy discussion as to the exact happenings of previous weddings in the Massey family, with a great many asides as to whether he intended to follow them to the letter.

She was rendered speechless when he said casually: 'Probably Katie and I will get married while we're in Greece, but if we do, I promise you we'll have a reception here when we get back.'

Which at least turned everyone's thoughts to Greece. Great-Uncle Tom, who had spent several holidays there, had a great deal to say about its history, and unfortunately addressed most of his remarks to Katrina, who beyond a vague knowledge of the Acropolis, Delphi and the beauties of the Aegean islands, was quite unable to cope with a flood of information about Greek gods and goddesses, Atalanta and the golden apples, Poseidon, Hestia and Demeter, Athena and Dionysus. They sounded to her ears to be a bloodthirsty lot. It was when Great-Uncle Tom started quoting bits of Greek to her that Lucius took pity on her and started a discussion with the old man about classical Greek, quoting bits back at him, to his uncle's great delight, and leaving her free to listen to Dora's gentle dissertation on catering for a wedding. It seemed that she hadn't taken Lucius's remarks about getting married in Greece seriously.

'A very pleasant family evening,' observed Lucius, driving her back later. 'I couldn't bear it more often than Christmas and Easter and the odd birthday,' he added as an afterthought. 'I suppose one would call the older ones a bit old-fashioned, but then I'm inclined to be that myself about some things.'

'What sort of things?' They were already turning into the drive from the lane, and Katrina wished they could have gone on driving for ever.

'Oh, marriage and children and wives and so on.' He stopped the car and she said quickly: 'Don't get out, there's Lovelace opening the door. Thank you for a lovely evening, Lucius.'

She had her hand on the door, but he leaned across and covered it with his own. 'Since when have I dropped you off like a sack of coal?' he asked, and got out, walking with her to the porch where Lovelace stood just inside the door. 'Tomorrow morning?' he bent and kissed her lightly. 'Sleep well, Katie.'

She was up early, pale from a wakeful night, aware that she wasn't looking her best in a morning which was not yet quite light. Lucius was already there when she reached the stables, saddling Gem. His good morning was cheerfully offhand, although the look he gave her was intent. They didn't say much as they set off. For years now they had formed the habit of riding in the early morning together, even in the cold and semi-dark of winter, and they knew each other far too well to need to make conversation. They were more silent than usual this morning, although once they were back and had handed the horses over to the boy, just arrived from the village, Lucius took her arm as they walked up to the house and said casually: 'In a couple of weeks' time we'll be in Greece. Looking forward to it?'

She was startled. 'Heavens, as soon as that? You've quite made up your mind to go?' She didn't quite know why she asked him that; it was a silly question, but for a moment she wished wildly that she need not see him for a long time; perhaps she would get over him then.

His grey eyes were suddenly cool. 'Cold feet?' His voice was as cool as his eyes.

'Certainly not! I—I'd forgotten how soon we were going. I'm looking forward to it.' She could hear the note of defiance in her voice and hastily added brightly: 'I'm really looking forward to it.'

And over breakfast she took care to talk about nothing else but their trip, not noticing Lucius's thoughtful look which presently turned to amusement.

When they'd finished their meal he got up to go. 'I'll fetch you this evening,' he told her in a voice which she had long ago recognised as not to be argued with. 'Have fun with Mrs Lovell.'

Katrina spoke before she thought. 'Mrs Lovell? Why should I . . . Oh, of course—lunch. I don't think she quite approves of us going away together.'

'Then you can spend a profitable time convincing her that everything will be strictly *comme il faut*.'

He was laughing at her and she didn't like it.

She had warned Mrs Beecham that she wouldn't be home for lunch or dinner. 'But I'll be back for tea,' she assured that lady. 'I'll have it in the sitting room, please, and lots of buttered toast.'

She changed and took Bouncer for a walk, then got into her car and drove away to her mythical lunch. Once out of the village she turned back towards the Banbury road, went through that town and on to Warmington, where she lunched in the bar of the Plough Inn. There were plenty of people there, mostly men having their pint before their dinner, and she felt conspicuous, but she stayed as long as she decently could, then got into the car again and drove back through country roads, through Wroxton and then out of her way to Chipping Norton and then slowly back to Tew.

It was half past three as she stopped outside her own front door, and she left the car there. If Lucius happened to be at his drawing room window or out in the park, he would see it easily, proof that she had been away, although she told herself robustly that there was no reason at all why she shouldn't do exactly what she liked with her days. All the same, going into the lamplit sitting room, she felt guilty. It had only been a small deception for the best of reasons, but she didn't lie easily, especially to Lucius.

He came, as always, punctually, and she wasn't quite ready. She had put on the patterned organza; there would be friends dropping in later in the evening and several guests for dinner as well as the Massey family, and she wanted to look her best. She added his gifts too and tripped downstairs feeling for once rather less plain than usual.

It was a pity that Lucius's casual greeting didn't include some pleasant remark about her appearance. Other than wanting to know if she had enjoyed her day, he had little to say as he drove her over to Stockley House. It was left to Great-Uncle Tom to give her a hearty kiss and declare that she looked a picture and he wished he was twenty years younger. Indeed, several people remarked on her looks, and the more who did, the prettier she felt. By the end of the evening she was positively radiant.

There had been dancing after dinner, with cars driving up every few minutes, bringing more friends and acquaintances. Quite a few of them Katrina didn't know—people from London, all of whom seemed to be on terms of the greatest friendliness with Lucius, especially several smart young women. She hated them on sight. Before she had discovered that she had fallen in love with Lucius, she would have looked at them with tolerance and curiosity but certainly no jealousy. Now she discovered that she was riddled with it, it added a pretty flush to her cheeks and a most becoming glitter to her beautiful eyes.

She danced without pause, slow-foxtrotting with Great-Uncle Tom, who danced with a complete disregard for the music, waltzing with little Tom and letting herself go with the younger members of the party. With Lucius she was all liveliness and chatter, so unlike herself that he first of all looked puzzled and then amused, presenting a bland face to her and answering her incoherent conversation with a silkiness that she didn't notice, so busy was she in presenting a carefree air of enjoyment of the evening. She had given evasive answers to his casual questions about her lunch with Mrs Lovell, not actually fibbing, she assured herself silently, just evading the truth. Rather successfully, she decided as the evening progressed and the champagne she had been drinking went to her sensible head.

Lucius drove her home soon after midnight. 'I'll come in', he said easily. 'Mrs Beecham's sure to have left some of her excellent coffee in the sitting room.' He added dryly: 'You could do with some.'

'Are you suggesting that I've had too much to drink?' asked Katrina, aware of the beginnings of a headache.

'Yes.' He took the key from her and opened the door and followed her into the hall. 'But I daresay you needed it.'

She paused on her way to the sitting room. 'What do you mean?'

He was lounging against the wall table, looking

at her. She didn't much like the look. 'Shall we have our coffee?' she asked.

He took no notice of that. He said very evenly: 'What did you have at the Plough, Katie? Something in a basket or a ploughman's lunch?'

She whisked round, her eyes wide. 'However did you know?' she demanded.

He smiled, not very nicely. 'I phoned Mrs Lovell to ask her if she would like to come back with you and have tea—it seemed a friendly gesture . . .' He began to walk towards her. 'She was utterly bewildered, poor woman: terrified that she'd invited you for lunch and forgotten all about it. I rang Lovelace, who said that you'd left by car and wouldn't be back until about four o'clock, so then I phoned Lady Ryder, Mrs Moffat . . .' he shrugged his shoulders, 'everyone who knows us. I tried the pubs next and struck lucky almost at once; you'd only just left.'

Katrina said in a choking voice: 'Spying on me! You've no right . . .'

'Lucius raised his eyebrows. 'But indeed I have, my dear. Surely old friends have a right to be concerned when one of their number takes herself off?' He put a hand under her chin, cupping it gently and forcing it up so that she had to look at him. 'What's happened?' he asked gently now. 'What could there possibly be that you felt you couldn't confide in me?'

Katrina had gone rather pale. 'I thought we were seeing too much of each other,' she stammered.

His eyes widened in mocking surprise. 'My dear girl, we've been seeing each other almost daily for twenty-five years or more. Why the sudden volte-face?'

She would have given anything in the world to have told him. She said in a bright voice: 'Silly of me, wasn't it? Shall we have that coffee?'

He followed her into the sitting room, accepted a cup and sat down opposite her. 'Riding tomorrow morning?' he asked pleasantly, and because she couldn't think of any reason why she shouldn't, she said yes.

'Everyone goes home tomorrow after lunch,' he went on, 'and I shall be in town for a few days. I've promised to look in on several people and I can put in some work during the days.'

All those smart young women. Katrina clamped her splendid teeth together and smiled at him. 'You deserve some fun after these last few days,' she said sweetly.

He put his cup down and got to his feet. 'I dislike sarcasm in women,' he observed bluntly. 'Their tongues are like kitchen knives, far too sharp.'

He crossed the room to where she was sitting, mouth slightly open, eyes wide, kissed her swiftly on the cheek and walked out. She listened to the front door closing after him. 'He didn't say goodnight,' she said to Bouncer dozing in front of the fire. She was quite unable to stop the flood of tears that poured down her cheeks. What with too much champagne and even more emotion, she was in no state to prevent them.

The last thought in her head before she slept was that nothing, just nothing, would make her ride with Lucius in the morning. She woke early and lay, longing to get up, listening to the early morning sounds in the house and outside. It was cold and quiet outside. She heard Lucius's great horse coming up the drive and then turning away to the stables, and presently she heard him trotting through the cobbled yard and out of the back drive. She thumped her pillows and rolled herself into a snug ball again. She wasn't going to get up; she had said goodbye to the Massey family on the previous evening and Lucius wouldn't dare come to breakfast.

In a little while Maudie came in with her tea and a request from Mrs Beecham as to whether she should cook breakfast for Mr Lucius.

'No, thank you, Maudie, he's going up to London for a few days—he won't have time. And could I have mine in half an hour? I've got some work to do and I want to get into the studio as quickly as possible.'

As Maudie reached the door: 'And if anyone calls or telephones, tell them I'm not here or can't come, or something, will you?'

She ate a hurried breakfast, with one ear tuned to Lucius's footsteps. But he didn't come, so she went straight to the studio and began work. It was a good thing she had already done the sketching, it was just a question of painting to be done, work she could do while most of her mind was engaged elsewhere. The morning wore on, and each time the door bell rang, and she heard its faint echo below her, and it rang often enough, she stopped painting, listening for Lucius's deliberate tread on the stairs. Only he didn't come. She had lunch presently, made a belated visit to the kitchen and then took Bouncer for a long walk. There were few lights shining from Stockley House as she came back through the kitchen gardens; it would be empty but for the servants. She turned away quickly and hurried back home to have her tea and then put the finishing touches to her work.

Normally she would have taken it up to London and handed it over to the publisher, but if she did there was just the chance that she might bump into Lucius and he would say something unpleasant about spying. Katrina ate her solitary dinner with a book propped up in front of her and went early to bed.

She had Mrs Moffat to lunch the next day, because she had promised flowers for the church and Mrs Moffat had been eager to come and fetch them herself. Katrina took her up to the greenhouses and stood by while Old John grudgingly parted with some chrysanthemums and a pot or two of cyclamens, and then bore her back to the sitting room to drink sherry and gossip gently until lunch was put on the table. It was a delicious meal, carefully chosen because Katrina knew that the Moffats lived simply and Mrs Moffat did her own cooking. One of Mrs Beecham's celery soups, beef en croûte and trifle to finish up with. Mrs Moffat, drinking the last of the claret and preparing to follow her hostess back to the sitting room for coffee, felt quite guilty, knowing that her husband would be sitting down to a pasty and the last of the Christmas pudding. She would have liked to have stayed, but there was the Mothers' Union at three o'clock and she got up reluctantly and then brightened when Katrina offered, with a disarming diffidence, a bottle of claret to take to the Vicar. 'To toast the New Year,' she explained. 'I expect you'll be at home, won't you? I've no idea what I'll be doing; Lucius may not be back, but if he is I'll be over at Stockley House.'

'But if he isn't, you'll be on your own . . .'

'I'll go up to London,' improvised Katrina rapidly.

When her guest had gone she allowed herself to wonder just what she would do if Lucius didn't come back. No one in the village did much in the way of entertaining at the New Year; small family parties, perhaps, but no entertainment for any one else. It was customary for Lucius to invite as many as would like to come to call in for a drink, and she and Virginia had always gone to Stockley for dinner on Old Year's Night and stayed to see the New Year in, simply because their parents had done it while his parents were alive and no one had thought of changing the habit. But now Virginia wasn't there and she had made Lucius angry. She got to her feet slowly, whistled to Bouncer and went for another walk.

It was early on Old Year's morning, while she was poking around in the shrubbery at the side of the house while Bouncer rooted happily beside her, that she heard the whisper of tyres coming up the front drive. Just for a moment she made as if to go and see who it was, but she had done that so many times during the last day or two, only to find that it was somebody other than Lucius; that she deliberately turned her back and began an inspection of a hamamelis; any day now it would bloom, and she loved the scent of its delicate lemon-tinted flowers.

Lucius came over the lawn, soundlessly, so that she wasn't aware of him until he fetched up within a few feet of her. She looked over her shoulder, her face suddenly radiant. 'Lucius—how absolutely marvellous!' She remembered the last time they had seen each other. 'I hope you had a nice time in London,' she said in a stiff little voice. It was a pity she was looking so scruffy in an old guernsey and corduroys and a pair of dreadful old boots she hadn't bothered to lace up. He must have thought the same, because he said, 'Hello there, what a nice change from the beautifully groomed young ladies I've been consorting with.' He grinned at her. 'And I did have a . . .' he paused, 'a nice time, thank you.'

They stared at each other for a long minute. 'And you,' he wanted to know, 'have you had a nice time too, guzzling ale at various pubs?'

The colour flamed into her cheeks. 'How beastly you are—you haven't changed a bit since you were a horrid boy!' Suddenly she felt laughter bubbling up inside her. 'You're impossible,' she giggled, 'but it's so hard to quarrel with you. I suppose it's because we've grown up together.'

'That probably accounts for it, there could be other reasons.' Lucius didn't say what they might be. 'Any chance of coffee?'

'Yes, of course, and Mrs Beecham made one of her fruit cakes yesterday—the Parish Council came to tea, but there's plenty left. You weren't here,' she added accusingly.

They were walking back to the house with Bouncer tearing ahead, showing off before the Dalmatian and the puppy.

'Oh, but you were quite capable of dealing with any number of parochial meetings,' Lucius observed easily. 'I've got two tickets for *Tosca* next Saturday evening. We'll dine somewhere first, shall we?' He gave her a quick sideways glance. 'Don't try and think of an excuse, Katie, and don't go fancying I've asked you as a sop to your pride because I've been taking a handful of girls out. None of them, by the way, would stomach opera. Oh, I daresay they go, because it's the thing to do, but they never allow their feelings to show, they might ruin their make-up.'

Katrina paused in the porch. 'You do sound bitter. Was there someone in particular? You danced a lot with that gorgeous blonde creature in the patterned chiffon . . .'

She spoke lightly, rather proud of her cool friendliness. That she was positively awash with misery at the very idea of him falling for a girl—any girl—was quite beside the point.

They were in the hall, throwing off their gloves and in Katrina's case, kicking off the deplorable boots. He turned to look at her, a half smile on his face. 'There's been someone particular for a very long time, Katie.'

She said impulsively: 'Then why do we have to go to Greece and pretend we're engaged? None of our friends would mind if they knew the truth—they'd laugh nicely and forget it. Besides, I don't mind it if they do laugh. The—the girl might mind.'

'Not she, she's too sensible.'

They went into the sitting room and Lovelace brought the coffee and the remains of the cake. Lucius ate almost all of it.

'Any news of the happy couple?' he asked presently.

'I had a card from—oh, dear, I can't remember. Lovely weather, Virginia said, but she didn't say when they were coming home.'

He nodded. 'You're coming this evening, as usual? There'll be a few people in for drinks, but only us two for dinner.'

Katrina looked surprised. 'Oh—you usually invite . . .'

His interruption was smooth. 'I thought it

would be nice if we were on our own this year.'
His eyes positively danced with amusement.
'Besides, we have the details of our trip to settle.'

He went shortly afterwards and she strolled off
to find Mrs Beecham and beg her to make another
cake. She had just changed into a sweater and skirt
when Lovelace came to tell her that Lady Ryder
had called, and she hurried downstairs to greet the
old lady.

'How very nice,' she exclaimed, and meant it.
'Would you like coffee, or perhaps a glass of
sherry?'

'Sherry, my dear. I read somewhere that the
elderly benefit greatly from the judicious drinking
of alcohol.'

She accepted the generous glassful she was
offered and sat back comfortably. 'And is the date
fixed?' She wanted to know.

'The date . . .? Oh, yes, of course—well, we
haven't decided yet.'

'I can't think why not, my dear. Lucius has a
good home and money and a flourishing job, has
he not? When do you go on this holiday?'

'In just over a week.'

'Of course, in my day such a thing was unheard of,
but times have changed. Young people seem to
consider marriage as a relatively unimportant thing.'

'I can assure you, Lady Ryder, that Lucius and I
think it's rather important.'

Katrina offered more sherry and passed the little
biscuits the old lady liked.

'I wonder why he was so attracted to Virginia?'
mused Lady Ryder aloud. 'Far too young for him,
though I admit a very pretty girl. Which is more
than you are, my dear, although you have style
and charm, which I consider far more important.'

Katrina finished her sherry and poured herself another; she felt she was going to need it. She had wondered so many times exactly the same thing, but unlike her guest, she hadn't the pluck to ask him. It would be one of those annoying topics to be mutually ignored for ever and ever.

'Virginia is pretty, isn't she?' she agreed in her pleasant voice. 'I'm so glad she's happy with James, I think they'll make a splendid couple.'

'Fiddle!' declared Lady Ryder sharply. 'Young Lovell is one of the dullest young men I've ever met; I'm not saying that they won't be happy, because he'll do exactly what Virginia wants him to.' She finished her sherry and helped herself to another biscuit. 'I hope you and Lucius intend to have a family; there is no excuse for not doing so. The house is large and so is his income; he will be able to provide you with every conceivable comfort and have the children educated properly.'

Katrina went bright pink, took a swallow of sherry and gasped. When she had finished coughing she said carefully: 'It is a large house, isn't it, but a very comfortable one. Children will fill it nicely.'

Lady Ryder prepared to go. 'I will be godmother to your first,' she said in a tone of satisfaction. 'But don't leave it too long, Katrina. I am not as young as I was.'

Katrina was left to digest this remark, standing in the porch after Lady Ryder had pecked her cheek in goodbye and got into her elderly car. She would dismiss all these silly ideas from her mind, she told herself briskly, and go for a good walk after lunch.

She was just sitting down to this meal when she heard the front door open and Lovelace's voice raised in welcoming tones. Lucius—and why had he come at such an awkward time? Bad news of someone in the village? Worse—something had happened to Virginia and James? She half rose from her chair as he came in on Lovelace's heels.

'I felt lonely,' he said. 'Will you invite me to lunch?'

It was a bit of an anticlimax. 'Yes, of course. Lovelace, please lay a place for Mr Lucius and ask Mrs Beecham if she could make another omelette.'

Lovelace beamed. Mr Lucius was behaving exactly as a young man in love should, he considered. No one in the kitchen, nor for that matter his own staff at Stockley House, had entertained for one moment the possibility of his engagement to Miss Virginia, whatever everyone in the village had thought. Now Miss Katrina was quite a different kettle of fish; they had already started a whip-round in both houses for the wedding present.

'And a bottle of that Sauternes Mr Lucius enjoys, Miss Katrina?' he enquired, quite sure she would say yes.

They dawdled over their meal, having their coffee at the table while Lucius drew neat little maps in his pocketbook of the area around Athens.

'We could, of course, rush from here to there, sightseeing every minute of the day and remembering nothing afterwards. I think it's a better idea if we keep to a small region and take our time. We can always go again.'

Katrina ignored the last bit. 'I'll have to do some reading. I don't know one Greek god from the next, only I do want to see the Parthenon.'

'And so you shall. We'll drive out early in the

morning before everyone else gets there. It's
magnificent. There are other temples just as fine,
but most of them too far away, but we can go out
to Sounion—stay there for a couple of days, if you
like.' He put down his coffee cup. 'I must go—I've
got the estate accounts to go over.' He went to the
door. 'I'll fetch you about seven o'clock.'

There were a lot more people there than Katrina
had expected, all old friends though and not a
smart woman in sight. Aware that she looked her
modest best in the brown velvet suit, she went the
rounds, glass in hand, exchanging local gossip,
answering with gentle vagueness when she was
asked when she and Lucius planned to get
married. 'Of course, we all knew all along that you
and Lucius would make a match of it, dear,'
declared Mrs Moffat fortunately with no one near
enough to hear this artless piece of information. 'I
mean—so suitable; old family friends and knowing
each other for a lifetime. You'll enjoy your holiday
together.' She eyed Katrina speculatively.

'I'm told that Greece is very romantic,' said
Katrina gravely.

After everyone had gone, they had dinner in the
small room at the back of the hall and afterwards
they sat round the drawing room fire, talking idly
until Cobb came in with champagne in a bucket,
followed by one of the maids with a tray of
glasses. For many years now it had been
customary for everyone at Stockley House to
assemble in the drawing room and toast the New
Year. Just before midnight they came in, one by
one, led by Cobb and strictly in order of seniority,
to stand in a semi-circle, glass in hand, while Cobb
stood poised ready to open the champagne. He
knew exactly the right moment. With the first

stroke of Big Ben he had the first bottle opened and was filling Katrina's glass and then Lucius's and then everyone else's in the room. He was ready with his glass in his hand as the last note of midnight struck and presently led his colleagues in good wishes and handshakes all round. Katrina, standing beside Lucius, envied him his easy good manners, saying just the right thing to everyone as he shook their hands. She could think of nothing more original to say than, 'A Happy New Year', to each of them.

It wasn't until they had all gone again, carrying the empty bottles and glasses with them, that Lucius bent to kiss her. 'And a happy new year to you, my dear,' he said lightly. He had wished her that in precisely the same fashion for years now; even his kiss was a brotherly peck.

She said brightly: 'And to you, Lucius.' She couldn't think of anything else to say.

He drove her back presently, going into the house with her but not stopping more than a few minutes. 'I must go up to town in the morning,' he told her, and she waited for him to offer her a lift as he often did. But this time he didn't. There would be no offices open, he wouldn't be going to do any work. It would be the lovely blonde, she supposed unhappily, the someone particular he had known for some time. She was amazed at the wild ideas streaming through her head; to go to London too and watch where he went, see this girl, find out where she lived, what she did. She was appalled at herself; if this was being in love then the quicker really she reverted to being Lucius's old friend the better. She wished him goodnight without mentioning his visit to London and watched the car going down the drive. If only she could meet someone—a man who would fall for her hook, line and sinker, and Lucius could return home to find him glued to her side. It wouldn't make any difference to Lucius's feelings, of course, but what a splendid boost it would give her downtrodden pride. It was a pity, but she couldn't think of a single man of her acquaintance who would fill the bill. There was no such man, she decided gloomily.

But there was. She met him the very next morning.

CHAPTER SEVEN

KATRINA had gone through the kitchen gardens and out through the wicket gate into the field beyond, Bouncer racing ahead, when she saw a man walking towards her. He paused as Bouncer paused too and growled, and she called: 'It's all right, he won't do anything unless I tell him to. You're trespassing.'

He came nearer and she was able to see that he was quite young, a little above middle height, with dark hair and eyes. 'So sorry,' he said easily. 'I'm lost—I'm staying a day or two with the Merediths. My name is Johnson—Pete Johnson.'

The Merediths lived in the next village, she knew them slightly. She smiled and said: 'You're about four miles from home, then. I'm Katrina Gibson, and I know the Merediths. I'm just going back for coffee; would you like a cup?'

He beamed at her. 'Rather! I'm dog tired, if you must know—spend my days in the city and never walk more than twenty yards at a time. "Go for a walk," they said, "and be back for lunch." I was lost within the first half hour!'

Katrina laughed. 'It's easy to take a wrong turning.' She had turned and was walking beside him and presently ushered him through the wicket gate past Old John's disapproving stare, into the kitchen gardens and across the lawn to the house.

'Nice place,' commented her companion, pausing to take in its pleasant exterior. 'How comfortably Regency folk lived, didn't they?'

'I suppose so. I've never lived anywhere else.'

He glanced at her. 'Lucky you. You're married, of course?'

It was impossible to take offence at his friendly tone. 'No, not yet—just engaged.'

'And you'll give up all this . . .?'

'Yes.' She turned and pointed to Stockley House, standing very stately among the bare winter trees a mile away. 'I'll be there instead.'

'I say, that's some place, isn't it?'

'It's very nice,' said Katrina sedately. 'Come on in and have that coffee.'

Lovelace came to meet her as they went indoors. 'This is a friend of Mr Meredith's who got lost out walking,' she told him. 'He's going to have coffee before he starts back.'

Lovelace inclined his head in disapproving civility. 'Yes, Miss Katrina. There was a telephone call from Mr Lucius. He asked if you would telephone him at your convenience.'

'Thanks, Lovelace.' She turned to her guest. 'Take off your coat, it's warm indoors.' And when he had done so and they were sitting in the drawing room: 'Are you just a friend of the Merediths or a relation?' She added apologetically: 'I don't know them very well.'

'A nephew—a distant one, though. I've not been to their house before. It's pleasant in these parts.'

They talked idly while they had coffee, not noting the gradual darkening of the room until Katrina exclaimed: 'My goodness, it's snowing—who'd have thought it!' She went to a window and peered out. 'You'll never get back in this, you'll have to stay for lunch. Give the Merediths a ring and just as soon as it clears I'll run you back in the car.'

She didn't listen to his protests. 'I'll be glad of your company,' she told him, and wished fleetingly that Lucius would walk in and find her entertaining this nice young man.

The snow didn't stop. It was long after lunch time and they were drinking their coffee round the fire, the best of friends, when Katrina glanced out of a window and saw that the sky was clearing and there was no more snow.

It was only as she was getting into the car that she remembered that she hadn't telephoned Lucius. It couldn't have been urgent or he would have rung again. She waved at Lovelace, standing austerely in the porch and started down the front drive. She was almost at the gate when the Bentley turned in from the lane and passed her. She had a glimpse of Lucius's face as she slid past him. He looked cross, a fact her companion remarked upon. 'I say, what a bad-tempered bloke in that Bentley—a mouth like a rat-trap and eyes like grey rock. Shouldn't like to get on the wrong side of him!'

Katrina negotiated the turn into the lane with care. 'My fiancé,' she said calmly, and added: 'I quite forgot to give him a ring.'

'Oh, lord! I say, shall we go back so that I can explain—apologise . . .'

'Certainly not. It's not in the least your fault, and by the time I'm back he'll have forgotten all about it.'

She was aware that this was wishful thinking on her part. Probably Lucius would be coldly sarcastic, downright nasty in fact. Serve him right for going to London so often. Two could play at that game, she told herself hearteningly.

It was a short drive to the Merediths' house, she could have been back home again in half an hour, but she allowed herself to be persuaded to stay for tea, and since Mrs Meredith was a chatty type who had a great deal to say about everything and everybody, half an hour stretched into an hour. Katrina made her excuses at last, made a half promise to see Peter again before he went back and edged her way out of the room, with her hostess, still talking about the Hunt Ball, beside her. 'And you're going to marry Lucius Massey, are you not, my dear? So very suitable—two old local families, you know. We shall look forward to the wedding.'

Katrina got into the car and drove home through the rapidly darkening afternoon. For some reason she was feeling peevish, perhaps because she disliked being considered suitable. Suitable for what? She brought the car to an untidy halt beside the Bentley. So Lucius was still waiting for her, was he? She went into the house prepared to be met with an icy stare and his most chilling voice.

When she went into the sitting room he was sitting by the fire, his long legs stretched out comfortably, a tea tray on the table beside him, the epitome of comfort and ease. He got up as she went in. 'Lovelace was kind enough to give me tea—you don't mind?'

'No, of course not. Why should I? He's been giving you meals in this house for as long as I can remember.'

His fine mouth twitched. 'Indeed yes. You spent a pleasant afternoon, I hope? The snow was unexpected. Local too, nothing the other side of Oxford.'

She sat down and he resumed his comfortable sprawl, content, it seemed, to say nothing more. After a minute or two Katrina said crossly: 'Why did you want me to phone you?' She added: 'I forgot.'

'Naturally. I managed to get tickets for that new show—the one we were talking about the other day.' He glanced at his watch. 'Unfortunately it starts at half past seven and it's now almost six o'clock.'

Katrina had forgotten that she was annoyed. 'Lucius, how lovely! I'll fly into something, we can be away in fifteen minutes—we might just do it.'

He looked at her, his eyes hard. 'Unfortunately,' he said blandly, 'I thought it was unlikely that you'd be free this evening, so I cancelled the seats.'

She stared at him. 'You what? You never . . .'

'Your grammar is appalling,' he told her, and added with a smugness which made her boil: 'Such a pity to waste them when there are so many people wanting to see the show.'

He sat back watching her, and she felt exactly as she used to feel when she was a small girl who had been in mischief and had rushed to tell him about it. Most of the time it had been her own fault, and Lucius had sat looking at her until she admitted that. Once she had, his sympathy was boundless.

She said defiantly: 'He's a nephew of the Merediths, staying with them. He was out walking and got lost—he was in the top field. I asked him back for coffee and we—we talked.' With sudden fierceness she added: 'He was nice—he didn't stare at me as though I was half-witted or look at my clothes as though they were all wrong . . .' She stopped appalled, for she hadn't meant a word of it.

'Meaning what?' asked Lucius quietly.

It seemed best to take no notice of his question. 'It snowed and I said I'd drive him back when it stopped, and I did.'

'The beginning of a beautiful friendship?' asked Lucius chattily.

'You are mean . . .'

'Nasty, vulgar, arrogant? Come off it, Katie, you're as green as grass when it comes to men, and if an old friend isn't allowed to keep an eye on you, who is?'

She thought sorrowfully that an old friend was all he was ever likely to be. 'I'm quite capable of looking after myself,' she told him with dignity.

'Is he staying long?' asked Lucius casually. 'You might take him round a bit.'

'He did suggest that we meet again. There's a week before we go away, isn't there, and it's always a bit dull for a little while after Christmas.'

'A very sound idea,' said Lucius smoothly, and she glanced at him suspiciously. He was displaying a volte-face she didn't quite like. But they seldom stayed bad friends for long: they sat comfortably by the fire talking until Lovelace came in to enquire if Mr Lucius would be staying to dinner.

'No,' said Katrina sunnily, remembering his bad temper, 'he won't. And I'll have mine on a tray, Lovelace. I'm going to work in the studio this evening.'

Lucius remained unmoved by this lack of hospitality. 'A drink before I go?' he asked mildly. She gave him a whisky and helped herself to sherry.

'Another commission?' he asked pleasantly.

She frowned down at her glass. 'Not exactly— just some ideas I want to try out.'

He heaved himself out of his chair. 'Riding tomorrow?' he wanted to know. 'I have to go over to the Home Farm again.' He added casually: 'You'll be back in plenty of time to spend the day with your new friend.'

'There you are, being beastly again!' burst out Katrina. 'Anyone would think you were jealous!'

She could have bitten out her tongue the moment she had said it.

'But of course I am,' he agreed equably. 'You are, to all intents and purposes, my fiancée.' He sauntered to the door. 'Goodnight, my dear, don't work too hard at those ideas of yours.'

Katrina watched him go, bristling with temper, vowing to herself that if Pete Johnson asked her to go out with him, she would, all day and every day.

Only she wasn't given the chance. Lucius rode over shortly after breakfast and there was no faulting his casual friendliness, nor did he even hint at their bickerings of the previous evening. They rode off to the Home Farm and had coffee in its large, old-fashioned kitchen, then Lucius went off to inspect some repairs to one of the barns. It took a long time, and when he returned he mentioned apologetically that he had intended riding on to see one of his gamekeepers, another mile or so away, and by the time he had dealt with whatever his business was there and Katrina had spent another hour in the kitchen with the gamekeeper's wife, drinking strong tea this time, it was gone one o'clock.

'We may as well have some bread and cheese at the Massey Arms,' suggested Lucius, 'and then cut across the park.'

So they ate their ploughman's lunch and drank

Guinness and then went home through the darkening afternoon, and when they reached the house it seemed natural enough for Katrina to have tea while she was there, and because she was a little tired, she dozed off, and didn't wake until Cobb came in with a message for Lucius. He gave it discreetly into Lucius's ear, and she didn't hear a word of it. Lucius said easily: 'Oh, hallo, you're awake again—I never knew such a girl for dropping off! I'll run you home,' he glanced at his watch. 'I'm expecting someone in about half an hour.'

He didn't engage her in further conversation or enlarge upon that. She got to her feet and went out to the car with him; she wished him a placid goodnight at her own door and went up to her room. It was vulgar to pry, but that didn't stop her going to the window with the fieldglasses and training them upon the well-lighted entrance of Stockley House. She didn't have to wait long; she saw the Bentley come round from the side of the house and Lucius get in and drive away. The station was in Chipping Norton some miles away, so she would have time to take a bath.

She was back wrapped in a dressing gown, with time to spare. The car's headlights flashed down the lane and into the grounds of Stockley House, and she had a splendid view of Lucius and a young woman getting out of it and going indoors. She dressed in a fine temper, made worse by the message she had had given her by Lovelace. Mr Peter Johnson, he had informed her in a disapproving voice, had telephoned during the afternoon and had wanted to meet her. He had telephoned again later and left no message.

Katrina whisked her mousey hair into a

semblance of tidiness and went down to dinner. Halfway through she was called to the phone.

'Katie?' enquired Lucius softly. 'Just in case you were wondering who it was I fetched from the station—one of my partner's secretaries with some important papers which needed my attention.'

Katrina drew a deep indignant breath. 'What makes you think . . .' she began.

'Dear girl, I've known you since you were an infant. I can, at times, hear your thoughts.'

'Not all of them,' she said quickly.

Lucius sounded as though he was laughing. 'It's a pity I can't see your face—you sound guilty! Goodnight, Katie.'

It was a pity that Pete Johnson didn't ring in the morning. She hung around after breakfast, hoping he would call, and then, unable to put it off any longer, she went down to the village to the Parish Council meeting, where she was kept until lunchtime, weighing the pros and cons of a jumble sale or a bring-and-buy morning in aid of the church tower fund. And when she escaped at last, Lucius was outside, leaning against her car. 'I walked,' he told her, 'so may I beg a lift home?'

She unlocked the car door. 'Of course.'

He took the keys from her. 'I'll drive. Will you come in for lunch?' And when she hesitated: 'I want your advice about End Cottages—old Miles in the end one needs a new roof. I'm wondering if it would be sensible to have all four done . . . the others aren't too bad, but they'll need re-tiling in a year or two and will probably cost twice as much by then.'

Katrina knew almost as much about the Stockley property as her own; they were still weighing the fors and againsts as they sat down to lunch, and once that meal was over, she agreed readily enough to go with him to look at the cottages.

It was a fine day, although cold, and they walked across the fields to the edge of the estate. The cottages looked charming against the winter sky, backed by bare trees and the tall iron fence which ringed the house; they had been carefully maintained and modernised without detracting from their age, and Katrina said now as they approached them, 'You'll have to do the lot, Lucius, otherwise the tiles will look odd—you might never be able to match them up if you wait to re-roof the other three.'

'Yes, I'd thought that too. Let's go and see old Miles.'

The old man had been the estate carpenter for his whole life and, now retired, was pleased to see them. They drank tea with him, explained about the roofs and started back across the fields. They were almost at the house when Lucius said casually, 'I met your Pete Johnson this morning— he was on his way to Chipping Sodbury to get the train back to town.'

Katrina hardly heard him. 'You might as well have the sitting rooms papered when you do the roofs . . .' She stopped. 'Has he gone back to London? And he's *not* mine!'

'No? He could have been.' Lucius sounded amused.

She said peevishly: 'Probably, if I'd been given the chance to see him again. But each time he phoned I was out.'

'Oh, hard luck,' said Lucius, and opened the yard door and ushered her in to the back to the house. 'I won't come to dinner,' he said cheerfully, even though he hadn't been asked. 'You'll want to start packing.'

Which was true. He gave her a drink and then drove her back to her own home, where she went up to her room and began to pack, just as he had suggested, folding the pretty clothes carefully and wondering if he would find her attractive in them, marvelling that until now she had never minded over-much whether he noticed what she was wearing or not. 'Love is a very peculiar thing,' she told Bouncer, watching her with suspicion as she hunted through her cupboards for swimsuits: neat, navy blue and lacking in all frivolity. She tucked them away in corners in her case and wondered if she should have bought something a bit more exciting. Then: 'No,' she addressed Bouncer once more, 'that wouldn't do at all; I'm not and never will be an exciting person, am I?'

Bouncer, to whom all beauty was skin deep, grinned and wagged his tail.

Katrina spent the next day putting her household in order, paying a hurried visit to Mrs Lovell to explain why she couldn't be home when James and Virginia got back, taking Bouncer for a walk which was much longer than usual, and presiding over the W.I. tea-party, an annual function which she had almost forgotten about. She had never really enjoyed it, because she was shy on such occasions, and this year it was worse than usual, for she had to sit through a spate of questions about herself and Lucius, accompanied by coy smiles and nods and a great many references to Virginia. She answered calmly, apparently un-ruffled, agreed pleasantly that her sister and James seemed to be ideally suited, agreed again that the same might be said of herself and Lucius and remained vague as to the date of her own wedding. The ladies went one by one, a little annoyed, and having discovered nothing they didn't already know, and she was on her way up to her studio when Lucius walked in, using the yard door.

His 'Hullo' was cheerful. 'Didn't dare come in through the front door,' he told her. 'I remembered at the last minute that it was your annual chat-up. Was it fun?'

Katrina paused, one hand on the banisters. 'No,' she told him crossly, 'it wasn't. Why are people so interested in us?'

'Nothing unusual,' he said easily. 'In a small village we know everybody's business, and if we don't then we pry and poke until we do. No harm intended.'

'No, I know that. It's just a bit—well, awkward.' She looked away from him. 'And it will be worse when we get back and they discover that we're not going to be married after all.'

'Not a bit of it. They would all rally round you with genuine sympathy. I'll be the black sheep— probably I'll have to go to the North Pole or the Gobi Desert and stay away for years while they forgive me.'

Katrina came down the stairs with a rush. 'Lucius, you don't mean that? You wouldn't have to go away? I couldn't . . .' She stopped just in time.

'You couldn't what?' asked Lucius lightly, although his eyes were intent on her face.

'Nothing.' She retreated backwards towards the staircase once more. After a moment of silence she said feverishly: 'I'm all ready to leave. I think I've remembered everything.'

Lucius lounged across to her. 'No last-minute phone calls?' he asked.

'No,' she said coldly, pretending to mis-understand him.

'Ah, well, I daresay he'll write. Does he know where we're going?'

'If by he you mean Pete Johnson—no, he doesn't. Why should he?'

To her annoyance he didn't answer. 'Mind you're ready by nine o'clock,' he observed. 'Now I must go—unlike you, I've several calls to make. 'Bye!'

Katrina didn't reply, only tossed her mousey head at him and started up the stairs. It amazed her that she could be so exasperated by someone she loved so overwhelmingly. She had taken but three steps when Lucius was beside her. Without a word he kissed her soundly and went as quickly as he had come, leaving her with her mouth open and no feelings at all except a great rush of love. Lucky, she told herself, that he wasn't there to see it.

She occupied her evening saying goodbye to Lovelace and Mrs Beecham, taking Bouncer for a walk even though it was dark and cold and checking that she had everything she might need for their journey. It would have been sense to have gone to bed early, but she dallied around the house, washed her hair, did her nails, checked everything once more—unusual for her; she was normally so calm and collected—and finally, far too late, went to bed.

She slept badly, waking from nightmares where she was struggling to get to the airport in time, running in slow motion as the plane took off with Lucius on board. She woke quite tired out and found Mrs Beecham pulling back the curtains and her early morning tea on her bedside table.

She got up and bathed and dressed quickly, ate a sketchy breakfast under Lovelace's anxious eye, and went out with Bouncer. It was still dark and cold, and when she looked across the valley she could see the lights from Stockley House streaming out on to the frosty lawns around it. A reassuring sight; at least Lucius would be up and ready to leave.

She went back indoors, did her rather pale face again, and very suitably dressed in her tweed dress and matching coat, expensive gloves and shoes, and went downstairs. Her luggage was ready in the hall, the Gucci overnight bag and the roomy case. At least Lucius would have no reason to grumble at her not being ready.

He arrived a few minutes later in the Jaguar, wished her a casual good morning, saw her luggage into the boot, said a few pleasant words to Lovelace, who worshipped him in a slavish way Katrina found quite unnecessary, and told her to get in. 'Masses of time,' he told her comfortably. 'We'll have coffee on the way. Have you got a book to read?'

She looked surprised. 'No—should I have?'

'There's always a wait between getting there and actually boarding the plane. Never mind, there's bound to be something at the airport.'

'Have you got a book?' she demanded.

Lucius smiled faintly. 'I've brought some work to do.'

So that was why he was anxious for her to find something to read! If he thought she intended to chatter for the entire journey, he couldn't have been more mistaken. She settled in beside him without another word, and beyond answering him when he remarked upon something, had nothing to say for herself until they stopped for coffee at the Fleet service station,

It was large and noisy, full of people, even at that hour of a midwinter morning. Lucius fetched coffee and they sat, surrounded by people making late breakfasts. Katrina averting her eyes from a plateful of bacon and eggs being eaten with gusto, caught Lucius's own eyes on her.

'You're very silent,' he observed. 'Sorry you're coming?'

'Certainly not! Why do you say that? I have no doubt that I shall enjoy myself enormously. Are we in good time?'

'Oh, lord, yes, I'll turn off at Staines and go through the reservoirs. There should be someone waiting to take the car. Once we've checked in the baggage we can sit and twiddle our thumbs for an hour or more.'

'You can always work,' she reminded him sweetly.

Heathrow was a hive of activity, full of people racing round looking for luggage, children, porters, while the seasoned travellers trod carelessly among them, knowing exactly where they were going, immaculate in their well cut suits and carrying their executive bags. Katrina, told to wait while Lucius and the porter checked in their luggage, found herself between two elderly ladies, one cosy, plump and cheerful, the other, clad in a sensible raincoat and a no-nonsense hat, a thin, frowning lady, prepared for the worst. She said across Katrina's front: 'Surely you can remember if you had your red hatbox with you, Addy? If you haven't got it now where is it?'

Addy's face was as trusting as a child's. 'Someone will find it and put it on the plane, Dora.'

'Rubbish!' declared Dora, and turned on Katrina. 'My sister is so careless,' she said crossly, and added fiercely: 'What do you suggest?'

'I really couldn't say,' said Katrina mildly. 'I travel very seldom, but surely there's some sort of information centre here? Couldn't you enquire what to do there?'

Both ladies spoke at once. 'Upstairs,' snapped the thin one. 'And who's to mind the luggage?'

'We can hardly expect this young lady to do anything,' said the cosy one. 'I'll go, Dora.'

'You will not! Perhaps this lady will mind our bags and we'll both go.'

'I'm travelling myself,' interposed Katrina, still mild, but firm, and heaved a sigh of relief as Lucius said from behind her: 'Some kind of trouble? Can I help?'

They both told him, speaking together. Katrina admired him for the way in which he sieved through their muddled words, told them to stay just where they were and disappeared.

'Your husband, my dear?' enquired the cosy lady.

'My fiancé.' Katrina smiled at the nice old dear. 'I'm sure he'll be able to sort things out for you.'

'He looks most dependable.' The faded blue eyes were wistful. 'I'm sure you'll be very happy.'

'Where are you going?' asked her sister. Katrina didn't particularly want to tell her, but there seemed no way out. 'Greece.'

'So are we. Is there no one else travelling with you?'

Katrina felt inclined to tell the busybody to mind her own business. She said briefly, 'No.'

'I don't approve of unmarried people going on holiday together,' began the lady, and was luckily interrupted by Lucius returning with the hatbox. He cut short their thanks with charm, took Katrina's arm and started for the stairs.

'How on earth did you manage to get entangled with those two old souls?' he wanted to know. 'I only left you for a few minutes!'

'One of them was rather sweet, and they just sort of surrounded me,' she explained.

'Well, thank heaven we shan't meet them again.' Lucius was leading her to the bookshop, his hand tucked under her elbow.

'Don't be too sure,' she told him. 'They're going to Greece too.'

She chose a book and went upstairs and had coffee till their flight was called. There was no sign of the two ladies; Lucius remarked hopefully that they were probably lost or sitting in some remote corner, arguing with each other. But they saw them presently. They were the last to board the plane and passed through the first class compartment to reach their seats. The cosy one smiled nicely, her sister stared and snorted.

'I don't think she likes us,' murmured Lucius. 'What have we done?'

'If you must know, we're going on holiday and we aren't married.'

He let out a crack of laughter. 'We could, of course, remedy that—there's an English church in Athens, we could have the banns called or whatever one does. Would you like to be a respectable married couple, Katie?'

He had laughed, so he was joking. Her heart ached, but she said lightly: 'Not particularly, thank you. And I don't think you'd find a couple more respectable-looking than us, so I don't think we need to worry.'

She gave him a cheerful smile which concealed her feelings very well.

They didn't talk during take-off and once they were airborne Katrina opened her paperback and Lucius took a handful of papers from a pocket and began making notes on them. They could have been a married couple, married long enough to enjoy each other's company without bothering to talk. She turned the pages of her book, not reading it at all, wondering if their holiday was going to be a success, wondering why Lucius had been so keen to take her with him, wondering what she should do when they got back home. She wasn't sure if it would be worse to see him each day and hide her love under a mask of friendship, or never to see him again.

'Lunch,' said Lucius in her ear. 'Is that book dull? You're not reading it.'

The meal was excellent and Lucius made her drink some wine with it, so that she became nicely drowsy and dozed off, to wake at once at his touch on her arm. 'We're coming down,' he told her, and fastened her seatbelt.

They went down slowly, going through cloud, so that the plane emerged and the sun seemed brilliant and the sea a Technicolor blue which didn't seem quite real. Katrina peered down at the ragged coastline and the land beneath her. Not much green, but there were trees, small white dots which she took to be houses, narrow ribbons of roads, and coming into view now, although some miles away, the city of Athens. She stared down, wishing for a cup of tea. It was, after all, after five o'clock.

As he so often did, Lucius read her thoughts. 'You were so sound asleep we decided not to wake you when they came round with the tea. You shall have it the moment we get to the hotel.'

She smiled at him gratefully. 'Lovely! Did I miss anything while I was asleep?'

'No. We've been above the cloud most of the way.'

They landed a few minutes later and were through Customs in another five minutes. As they emerged into the entrance hall, Katrina said: 'Nice and quick, but a bit terse, didn't you think?'

Lucius took her arm. 'It's the language, I expect. Where's our porter? We'll get a taxi.' He grinned down at her. 'I hope you feel you're on holiday, because I do!'

CHAPTER EIGHT

THE Grande Bretagne Hotel was quietly luxurious, and Katrina's room, large and airy with a bathroom adjoining it, had a shaded balcony, complete with table and chairs. There was a sitting room dividing her room from Lucius's, and before she had unzipped her overnight bag he had called across from his own balcony.

'There's tea waiting for you. Come and have it now and tidy up later.'

Before she did so she went out on to the balcony. It overlooked a large square and a view of distant hills beyond orange trees. The air was clear and cool, but the sun and the blue sky made it seem to be much warmer than it was.

'Not warm enough to wear the things I brought,' she told Lucius as they sat over their tea.

'I've just been told that it's a good deal warmer than usual for the time of year, and they're expecting it to be even warmer. It's fifteen degrees today, but it will probably warm up to eighteen.'

'But isn't that rather unusual? It's only January.'

'Yes, it is, but it's very much to our advantage. Are you too tired to go out this evening? I thought we might go to the Acropolis tomorrow, fairly early in the morning, and then potter gently for the rest of the day. I'll hire a car and we'll go along the coast in a day or so. If you can be sufficiently spartan we might swim once in a while.'

Katrina put down her tea-cup. 'In January?' she

147

demanded. 'You must be mad! I've brought my swimsuit, though.'

'It's not too cold in the water even in January—worth a try anyway.'

She got up. 'Well, I'm going to unpack and change. Will you be here?'

He gave her a faintly mocking glance. 'Of course. We'll have a drink downstairs and have dinner later. Then our walk later too, perhaps?'

She nodded and went back to her room to bath and change into one of the knitted dresses and jackets she had packed. It was fine and silky and a pretty mushroom pink. Just for once she was satisfied with her appearance as she went back to the sitting room.

Lucius was on the balcony, but he turned to study her as she went in. 'Nice,' he observed. 'You deserve a champagne cocktail.'

The bar was elegant, busy and almost full, although there didn't appear to be many tourists there. They had their drinks and then went in to dinner, and although the restaurant was almost full, they were shown to a table by the window, so placed that they could scan the room as well as look out on to Syntagma Square, its pavements covered by café tables and chairs and kiosks selling newspapers and dozens of other useful odds and ends. Katrina turned away from the bustle outside to study the menu, ready to take Lucius's advice.

'Hors d'oeuvres, I think,' he counselled her, 'then moussaka and I should have an ice if I were you, but have cheese if you'd rather. Would you like to try the local wine?'

'Well, of course,' said Katrina, quite astonished. 'I mean, when in Rome . . .'

He smiled gently at her and she looked away, because when he smiled like that she found it hard to play the part of an old familiar friend.

She didn't like the wine very much, but the food was good, served by a cheerful waiter, who stopped to talk each time he came to their table. It surprised her when Lucius spoke to him in Greek, and the man, delighted, answered at length.

'Aren't you clever?' said Katrina when the waiter had gone. 'Were you saying much, or was it just passing the time of day?'

'That and finding out which is the best place from which to hire a car and what the roads are like inland.'

'And are they good?'

'Surprisingly, yes. There's not been nearly as much rain as usual, in fact, the weather's been exceptional; much warmer than it should be. He says the old people in the country don't like it at all; they think that it might mean storms later.'

'Well, I'm glad it's fine for us.' Katrina finished her coffee and went to fetch the light angora coat she had brought with her and went out into the square with him. It was crowded now and almost all the café chairs were filled under the lights. They strolled across to the war memorial beyond the orange trees and above the square, skirted the Royal Palace and went into the Royal Gardens, still open. It was too early in the year for flowers, but there were shrubs and juniper trees and tall cypresses.

'How long shall we be here?' asked Katrina.

'Two days, perhaps three. We'll stop another day as we return, if you like.'

She sensed that he wasn't very enthusiastic. 'If you don't want to, then I don't either,' she declared. 'There must be heaps to see in the country around.'

He smiled a little. 'There is. It would take months. But we'll skim the cream off this corner of the country in the time we have.'

She looked at him curiously. 'You've been here before, I know—how many times?'

'Four—no, five, and each time I return home I give thanks for the peace and quiet.'

'Well, it's noisy, but I think I like it—orange trees, you know, and being quite warm in January, and those mountains in the distance.'

She tucked a hand under his arm, because she had always done so and if she didn't he might notice. 'You can improve my mind with a few Greek gods,' she suggested.

They filled the next two days to overflowing. The Acropolis, naturally enough, took up their entire first morning. Katrina went happily up the sloping, slippery cobbles of the Sacred Way and stood gazing up at the Parthenon while Lucius pointed out the distant sea and the smoke of Piraeus, then turned her to view the whole of the Attic plain before showing her the Temple of the Wingless Victory, a charming miniature temple facing the Parthenon and very much to her taste.

There were few people about; it was still fairly early in the morning, but already the sun was unseasonably warm. They wandered from temple to temple and then looked round the Acropolis Museum, a sketchy visit, for it was by then more than time for lunch.

They went back to their hired car and Lucius drove to the Dionysos Restaurant, opposite the restored theatre of that name, and they ate pilaff, and vegetables stuffed with rice and herbs. Lucius ordered retsina for Katrina to try, but after one cautious sip, she wrinkled her ordinary little nose and declared that it tasted of turpentine, so he chose a sweet Samian wine for her, drinking the retsina with apparent enjoyment himself.

They spent the afternoon visiting the various monuments in the city, and if Lucius was bored he showed no sign of it, but explained patiently about the Tower of the Winds, the Gateway of Athena Archegetos and Hadrian's library before taking her into a confectioners to give her tea and the richest cream cakes she had ever set eyes on, and then, finally, the Byzantine cathedral, small and beautiful, putting to shame the great pile of the nineteenth-century official cathedral beside it. And after that, they drove back to the hotel to bath and change and share drinks in the sitting room before dinner.

'A lovely day,' declared Katrina. 'What are we doing tomorrow?'

'The Plaka, the old town, and we shall walk, dear girl. There won't be many tourists and we can roam at will.'

They went down to dinner presently and afterwards Lucius took her into the square, where they sat at a café table on the pavement and drank cups of thick strong coffee. It wasn't cold—chilly, perhaps, but not unpleasant.

Lucius took her through the Plaka the next day, through the narrow alleys, past tiny houses, to give her lunch at a taverna—vegetables and rice cooked in oil, Greek beer and a sweet sticky pudding for Katrina, and after they had eaten he took her to a small paved garden of cypress trees and shrubs where they sat in the afternoon sunshine, not saying much. As they got up to go Lucius asked:

'Enjoying it, Katie?' And when she said yes with all the fervour of a small girl, he kissed her gently.

It took all her will power not to kiss him in return.

They went shopping in the afternoon, to buy cards for Lovelace and Mrs Beecham and Mrs Lovell and Mrs Moffat, and Katrina bought bright embroidery to take home as gifts, and when they reached Syntagma Square again with its boutiques, Lucius bought her a small ikon. 'A little something to remind you of our holiday together,' he told her, and she thanked him with just the right note of pleasure in her quiet voice, thinking to herself that she wouldn't need an ikon or anything else to remind her, but she couldn't tell him that.

They had tea in another café and wandered back to the hotel, to follow the pattern of the previous evening. Katrina, packing her case once more ready for their leaving in the morning, wasted a good deal of time on her balcony watching the lively square below.

'Let's go out for a drink,' said Lucius from his balcony. 'I know we've had one already, but I'm not sleepy, are you?'

She denied tiredness and ten minutes later they were seated at a café table, coffee and brandy before them. Katrina hadn't really wanted the brandy, but Lucius had laughed at her 'Live dangerously,' he advised her.

She was lifting the glass to her lips when a voice said: 'How nice to see you again, my dear!'

The cosy little lady from the airport was standing by their table, smiling. Her sister was beside her, scowling. Lucius got to his feet, and wished them good evening and the cosy lady burst into speech. 'It's all wonderful, isn't it?' she wanted to know. 'We're in a pension, but we thought we'd see how the other half live.' She laughed cheerfully, but she looked wistful.

'Will you have coffee or a drink?' asked Lucius, and Katrina could have hugged him for the nice way he smiled.

'Thank you, no.' The cosy lady's sister spoke before she could answer. 'We aren't used to being out so late, we must get back to our rooms.' She looked disapprovingly at their glasses on the table. 'We don't touch strong drink. Good evening.'

She caught her sister by the arm and marched her away, and Katrina said: 'Poor old thing, I'm sure she'd have loved a drink.'

Lucius sat down again. 'I agree, but I'd have offered that sister of hers vinegar!'

They settled down again and were soon discussing where they should go first the next day.

They left after breakfast, taking the busy road to Piraeus and then making their way through the town and on to the coast road to Sounion. Piraeus was uninteresting, full of factories and foundries, and they made short work of it, glad to be on the corniche with the sea on one side and low-lying ground on the other, with tavernas here and there. The racecourse came next, then the airport, and after that the beaches with their fashionable bungalows and tavernas and presently, further along the coast, hotels, and then finally Sounion, the Temple of Poseidon high above the sea on the cliff edge.

They had coffee in the cafe at the foot of the temple and then climbed up the rough path to examine it better and stand and admire the magnificent view from the cliff top. It was a clear day. Lucius pointed out Milos, far away on the horizon, and since the sun was warm, they sat for a while idly in its rays, talking about nothing much, content with each other's company.

They went back to the hotel presently and had lunch, then drove on up the coast towards Lavrion with its mines and then up and over the steep pass and on to the Mesogeia plain. Here the country was different, with olive groves and a background of distant snow-capped mountains and villages whose ancient history Lucius patiently told her, stopping often to admire the view and then turning away to see Marathon Bay and drink tea and eat small sweet cakes at a roadside taverna. It was early evening when they reached Kophisia, and Katrina was surprised to find that they weren't so very far from Athens, but they had gone slowly, turning down side roads and making a wide sweep to the north of Kephisia, coming down to it through terraced vineyards and olive groves. Katrina, her head over-full with Greek mythology, was secretly glad to see modern villas amongst the trees and to discover that their hotel was modern too, with large rooms and showers and an excellent restaurant. All the same, even though she was tired, she had loved every moment of her day. 'One should really walk,' she told Lucius, 'to see everything in slow motion.'

He agreed and laughed at her. 'I've stuffed you too full, haven't I?' He passed his cup for their after-dinner coffee. 'Shall we stay here for another night?'

She was quick to say no; she knew his plans by heart and didn't mean to be the cause of him altering them. 'We're going to Thebes tomorrow,' she reminded him, 'and spending the night at . . .' she paused to get it right, 'Levadia.'

She slept dreamlessly and got up to another bright day. 'Too warm,' the old waiter told them over their breakfast, shaking his head worriedly.

'Well, I hope it lasts,' Katrina observed happily. 'I do want to swim just once.' She drank the last of her coffee. 'I'm ready when you are, Lucius.'

'Proper little slavedriver, aren't you?' he smiled. 'Are you going to nag me like this when we get back home?'

She smiled and shook her head and didn't trust herself to answer him.

Thebes disappointed her; it was ordinary, and as Lucius drove up the hilly main street, she wondered why they had come. As usual he read her thoughts. 'Not what you expected, is it? But its history is quite out of the ordinary and very bloodthirsty. I shan't tell you all of it, just the bare bones . . .'

Which he did over coffee at one of the tavernas in the main street. 'Levadia is our goal for the night, but we'll go off the road to see the more interesting sights and we'll take the longer route through Ptoion and Gla.'

Katrina murmured agreement. She had no idea where she was or quite where they were heading for; she had looked up their day's journey the day before and thought she had learned the route pretty well. Obviously she hadn't, but she was content to sit beside Lucius and listen to his quiet voice pronouncing Greek names without difficulty and know that however stupid her question, she would get an answer. Like a teacher with a dim pupil.

She asked: 'Don't you find it a bit of a bore, having me here? I don't know anything . . .'

He turned the car on to an ill-surfaced road and began an uphill climb. 'No, you're never a bore, Katie, and I enjoy telling you things.' He glanced sideways at her and smiled. 'I seem to remember telling you things from the moment I realised that you'd listen to me. How old would you have been, I wonder? Four—five?'

'About four,' she agreed gruffly, and remembered how she had worshipped him as a small child. The worship had altered into an unshakable friendship as she grew older, not even Virginia's nonsense had shaken it deep down, and now her love for him mustn't shake it either.

They reached Levadia in the late afternoon, after a stop to visit a Byzantine church on the way, not only very old, but there was an interesting story about it during the second world war which somehow stuck in Katrina's head more than its ancient history. There was a taverna close by and they had tea there, and the sweet cakes she was beginning to like.

She liked Levadia at once, spread out over the hills with spruce-covered mountains shielding its back and Mount Parnassus, snow-capped, towering in the distance. There was a lot of colour too, for the local industry was blanket-making and they hung, in every possible colour, from the house balconies.

Their hotel was simple, with sparsely furnished rooms and a shared shower, but it was clean, and away from the bustle of the main street. The food was excellent, and they followed their now usual practice of strolling in the evening and having coffee at one of the tavernas, watching the hustle going on around them.

'Delphi tomorrow and then we'll work our way

round Mount Parnassus and find some small village.' He studied her with thoughtful eyes. 'We might talk there, Katie?'

She just stopped herself in time from asking what about. Instead she said lightly: 'That sounds fun. I take it there's a lot to see in Delphi? Everyone I've met who's been there has said they simply must go there again.'

'There's a great deal to see. You can decide at the end of tomorrow if you want to spend more time there. Do you feel like a walk? There's a castle and a stream with some rather pretty scenery.'

She reflected, as she got ready for bed later, how well they suited each other, but perhaps that wasn't what Lucius wanted. Someone pretty, beautiful even, who wore couture clothes and had masses of small talk, whereas she had to be urged to buy the right clothes, and was more inclined to long comfortable silences when they were together than chatter. Besides, there was no getting away from the fact that she was quite lacking in looks. Lucius had said that he wanted to talk; he would want to tell her what he intended doing when he got back, she supposed. He might even be going to tell her about this girl he intended to marry—that was what old friends were for, to be confided in.

They left for Delphi directly after an early breakfast the next morning, Lucius regaling her with a few bloodthirsty legends as they went. They travelled westward through a strangely still morning, unseasonably warm and hazy and windless. They went through lonely country with mountains all around them, which Katrina assured herself firmly was why she felt strangely uneasy.

They stopped briefly to look at the monastery of

Hosias Loukas and drink coffee in the small hotel close by, then they went on again through almond orchards already in bloom and small fields, but these gave way to olive groves as they climbed steadily until they reached Arachova, where they stopped for an early lunch before driving on to Delphi, downhill now through a narrowing gorge. There were several hotels and a surprising number of shops. Katrina, agog to have a look round, was pleased when Lucius stopped outside one of the larger hotels, booked them in, parked the car and professed himself ready to take a walk. He stayed patiently beside her while she peered at embroidery, fleecy hearthrugs and woollen bags and then took her back to the hotel for tea.

'It's five minutes' walk to the Sanctuary of Apollo,' he observed when they had finished. 'Shall we take a stroll before dinner?'

The Sanctuary was almost encircled by cliffs and the Sacred Way was steep and narrow and hairpin bent, and the whole place was scattered over a number of ledges. Katrina was disappointed, adding practically: 'Though I expect that's because I know almost nothing about it—I daresay a student of Greek mythology would find it very interesting.'

Lucius agreed, at his most placid, and suggested that she might prefer the theatre. They climbed the stone stairs, and here she wasn't disappointed. The mountains around reflected the setting sun and it was very quiet. 'This is nice,' she said quietly, 'and it looks peaceful.'

Lucius took her arm. 'There's time to climb a little higher to the Stadium,' and the view was even better from there. They stood side by side, not saying much, and then took a short cut back to the village and the hotel. Half way down he stopped and turned her round to look at him.

'You like it? Could you live here?'

'Heavens, no!' And then because she thought that she had spoken too baldly: 'What I mean is,' she said carefully, 'it's utterly beautiful, but it's not like home—and its history is so violent . . .'

'You would be content to live in Tew for the rest of your days?'

She considered. 'Yes, but I'd want to go to London sometimes and perhaps go on holiday abroad, but I think I'd want to live in Tew for always.' She sighed. 'I'm dull, aren't I? And not clever enough to appreciate all this. I can't think why you asked me to come . . .'

He smiled a little. 'I did ask you to come, if you remember, Katie.' And she had to be content with that; if he had refuted her suggestion that she was dull and not clever it would have been nice, but after all he was an old friend and had no need to pretend to her.

They went on down the path and presently had dinner, and for the first time Lucius gave her a glass of ouzo to drink. She screwed up her face after the first sip and gave it back to him. 'It's a bit . . .' she began, not wishing to appear ungracious.

'An acquired taste. Have a glass of wine instead. Shall we spend another day here, or would you rather go on up into the mountains?'

Katrina had had her fill of ruined temples and Greek legends, for the moment at any rate. She had enjoyed every minute of it so far but hadn't had time to digest everything. She said, watching his face carefully for signs of annoyance: 'Well, I think that would be rather nice—if we come back this way we could stop and see the rest.'

Lucius's mouth twitched. The idea of cramming Delphi into an hour or so's visit amused him, but his amusement was gentle and kindly. 'That seems like a very sensible idea, Katie—we'll do that.' He glanced out of the window at the clear sky. 'The landlord says it will be fine again tomorrow and much too warm for the time of year. We'll leave after breakfast and see how far we can go.'

They got the obliging landlord to make them up a picnic before they set out, and he came to the door to see them off. 'Not good weather,' he frowned. 'You should keep to the road. There is a good taverna at Gravia where they will give you beds and food. You plan to come back by the big road?'

Lucius got into the car. 'We thought we might go back to Athens on the Eleana road, probably you'll see us again in a couple of days.'

The road climbed steeply, high mountains on either side, the road becoming narrow, screened by firs, wild pears and plane trees. They stopped for coffee in Amphissa and then went on to Gavia, where they took rooms for the night, had more coffee and then, because it was warm, got into the car again and went on along the narrow road until they found rough grass between the trees and a sheltered spot amongst the rocks and shrubs.

'It's a strange sky,' said Katrina as they spread their picnic. 'It looks brassy—do you suppose there'll be a storm?' She looked around her uneasily. 'It's so quiet.'

'Well, we are quite a few miles from the village and there's nothing much around us. Shepherds' huts in the hills, I daresay, and not many of those. But it is strangely quiet—no wind and this haze

. . .' He smiled reassuringly at her. 'It makes a change from rain or snow.'

They ate their bread and goat's cheese and fruit and shared the bottle of wine Lucius had put in the car, and all the while Katrina was aware that Lucius was only waiting for her to give him her full attention. She spun out her roll and cheese and then took much longer than she needed to packing up the remains of the food and the wine, but at last she sat back against a convenient boulder and said, 'You wanted to talk, Lucius.'

He gave her a long, considered look. 'That's right, and I've waited until we found a spot where there would be no distractions, so that you'll listen to what I have to say with your whole head and heart.'

She felt sick and wished she hadn't eaten all that cheese. She said carefully: 'Is it so important?' and then before he could answer: 'Perhaps I can guess . . . You did say . . .' She stopped on a gasp. The ground beneath her was moving, a gentle shudder so brief that she thought she had imagined it, and at the same instant Lucius was on his feet, pulling her to hers, his hand gripping her arm so hard that she winced, urging her at a run to where the grass had spread, rock-free and away from the trees, into a shallow bowl. He pushed her down on to the ground without ceremony and flung an arm around her as the grass heaved again under them. Katrina could feel the waves of movement surging up and subsiding again. Her voice came out in a squeak she strove to keep steady. 'An earthquake?' she managed.

'Yes, love. Just keep still and if I tell you to do something, do it without wasting time. If it gets no worse than this, we'll be quite all right.'

Nothing happened for perhaps five minutes; there was an uncanny stillness all around them which Katrina found nerve-racking. If she hadn't had Lucius with her, she thought, she would have had screaming hysterics.

The next tremor was longer and stronger and a few boulders came tumbling down, and at the same time she became aware of a kind of subdued roaring from somewhere beneath her. It grew louder and she realised that it wasn't beneath her any more but somewhere close by. She had had her face buried in Lucius's shoulder, now she dared to lift it cautiously and fearfully peer around her. Not far away, perhaps a quarter of a mile, the foothills they had driven through were sliding gently away, rather like a blancmange which hadn't quite set. She watched their progress in speechless horror.

'Is that going to happen to us?' she managed.

She had to admire Lucius's calm voice. Did nothing, she wondered wildly, ever shake his calm?

'No, because we're going to move back, up the hill, on to the road. The tremors are going east to west, and the road runs north to south, so we may escape the worst of it. When I say get up and run, do just that, darling, make for our picnic spot and then the road.'

'Will we be able to drive?'

She heard him laugh softly. 'Very unlikely—I think we may have to walk.'

Katrina thanked heaven silently that she was wearing flat easy shoes—and then swallowed back the nausea as another tremor, like a giant slow moving wave, sent more boulders tumbling, but she got to her feet when Lucius said, 'Now!' and ran blindly, her hand in his, back through the rough ground, luckily still once more.

They gained the road and found the car at a crazy angle, one wheel smashed by a fair-sized boulder. There was nothing in it that they needed; they had their passports and money with them and the basket holding their picnic had rolled away.

'Are we going to walk?' asked Katrina, knowing quite well that there was nothing else to do anyway. 'Is it far?'

A silly question; they must have come at least six or seven miles from the village of Gravia. Fortunately, it was downhill.

Lucius sounded comfortably reassuring. 'Not very, and I think it may have missed the town to a large extent.' He turned her round and looked at her up and down. 'Are you all right?' His voice dared her to be anything else, so she said in a still shaky voice: 'Of course I am.' But she was glad of his hand.

The road had been blotted out in places and they had to work their way round it here and there where there were deep fissures in the ground which Katrina found frightening, although she didn't say so. They had been walking for about half an hour when there was another tremor and Lucius pulled her quite roughly to the ground and flung an arm around her. She hadn't said anything, but she was shaking with fright and he bent and kissed her gently. 'Poor darling, are you very frightened?'

'Not if you're here,' she said, and instantly wished she hadn't said it. It mystified her very much when he muttered something about not the time nor the place, and as the world quietened down once more, dragged her to her feet and hurried her on again.

The road seemed endless and twice as long by reason of the side-tracking they had to do. Katrina lost all track of time; she was thirsty and tired and hot, and she didn't allow herself to think what they would do if Gravia had been damaged and there was no hotel. She could have cried with relief when Lucius paused at a bend in the road and said: 'Good, there doesn't seem to be much damage,' and pointed to the scatter of houses below them, still a good mile away. But what was a mile with tea and the chance of a bath at the end of it? Katrina kept up a good pace and then faltered a little as they reached the main street. Gravia had missed the worst of the earthquake, but it had been damaged. There were cracks in house walls, sagging roofs and a broken water pipe, and some of the shops had had their merchandise spilled across the pavement as though a giant vandal had been on the rampage. But the hotel was almost intact; true, there were a good many tiles missing and the door sagged alarmingly, but the landlord came hurrying to meet them, pouring out excited comments.

Lucius put Katrina into a chair and listened, translating as best he could. 'The worst of it missed this area, but there's some damage; the railway is blocked, so is the road, he thinks. There's no water; it has to be fetched from that bust pipe we've just passed. One or two people are injured, but none seriously, and he advises us to sleep out of doors tonight. He'll get us a meal as soon as he can and boil some water for you to have tea or coffee. Our baggage is safe, so if you want to clean up I should, just as soon as we've had a drink.'

Katrina nodded. She was tired still, but her

sensible nature was coming to the fore. 'Do you suppose we might help with some of the clearing up? I don't suppose we'll be able to leave here for a bit, shall we?'

For answer he came over to where she was sitting and bent to kiss her, quite fiercely this time. 'You're a jewel, my darling! I can't think of a single girl of my acquaintance who wouldn't either be having hysterics or wanting to make up her face and wash her hair.'

Katrina tried not to dwell on the kiss. She said soberly: 'I think I could have hysterics quite easily.'

'Don't dare. Here's tea, drink it up like a good girl. I'll be around when you get back here.'

She eyed him nervously. 'Yes, but suppose there's another tremor?'

'I'll be here.' His smile was so tender that she turned away and almost ran to her room.

Someone had fetched water, so she did the best she could, put on slacks and a thin sweater and hurried back to the front of the hotel. There were a lot of people in the street, carrying bedding into the olive groves at the end of the town, sweeping up debris, hammering up broken windows and doors. There was no telephone, Lucius told her, and it would take some time before they knew how bad the earthquake had been. It would have missed Athens and the coast and it was to be hoped, done most damage in the mountains where there were few people and even fewer villages. 'The tavernas are going to feed everyone presently; there's no electricity, of course, but one or two oil stoves undamaged.'

'What can I do to help?'

'Help feed the children, I should think—I'll ask.'

It was a job which needed no knowledge of Greek. Katrina helped out where she could and wished she could have done more. Lucius was shovelling rubble with some of the other men and the older women were still carrying blankets out into the open ready for the night. The worst was over, the landlord told them, the weather was already cooler and the sky had lost its haziness; now all would be well and they would be able to resume their holiday in a day or two. A pity about the car, he shrugged, but what could one expect?

Anything, apparently, thought Katrina, and wondered how they would get back to Athens. But she didn't bother Lucius with questions, he wouldn't know the answers anyway and he was far too busy. They had supper with everyone else later and presently, urged on by the landlord, took their blankets and pillows down the street and spread them out on the rough grass like everyone else. It was very crowded and extremely noisy, but Katrina was too tired to mind about that, only just before she slept she stretched out a hand to Lucius beside her. 'If you don't mind,' she told him, 'I'd like to hold your hand.'

His large firm grip was reassuring, as was his voice bidding her goodnight, and she was asleep within seconds.

They were in Gravia two days, and since they couldn't get away, they turned to with a will and helped where they could. Katrina helped with the cooking and the washing of dishes and the cleaning of houses, and suspected that Lucius was enjoying himself. Speaking the language helped, of course. Katrina, using sign language and head-nodding and shaking, envied him that.

At the end of the second day an army jeep came

through, bringing aid of all kinds and the news that the road was passable with great care, and since most of its occupants were to stay in Gravia to organise the clearing up, and the driver was to return to Athens immediately, Lucius and Katrina were offered a lift. They were given a rousing send-off as the jeep started on its return trip, and Katrina felt tears running down her cheeks as they turned a corner and the last of the houses was lost to sight. Lucius passed her his handkerchief, gave her time to mop her face, blow her nose and give a good sniff before remarking that they might return some day and renew acquaintance with the little town. He took the handkerchief from her, tucked her hand in his, and engaged in conversation with the driver until they reached Delphi, almost undamaged. Katrina hoped that he wouldn't suggest that they stop there, but he didn't, and they drove on over an increasingly better road and presently reached Athens.

The earthquake had been a mere tremor in the city and there had been no damage. Their driver set them down outside the Grande Bretagne, bade them a cheerful goodbye, and drove off as the doorman came down the steps to meet them and summon a porter to take their bags. Katrina could only understand a small part of what he was saying, his English was fragmental and heavily interlarded with Greek, but there was no mistaking the welcome they received from the hotel manager when they reached the foyer. Katrina, led to her room with a tray of tea carried hard on her heels, peeled off her clothes, drank her tea and soaked in a hot bath, thinking of the food she was going to eat presently. It was heavenly to get into one of her pretty knitted outfits and spend time on her face and hair and then go through to the sitting room where Lucius was waiting with drinks. 'It seems like a dream,' she observed, sipping sherry, and marvelled at Lucius's elegance—twenty-four hours ago he had been shovelling away a tumbled wall, covered in dust, sleeves rolled up and exchanging jokes with the man he had been working with.

'Bad in places, but on the whole, very nice.' Lucius stared at her so hard that she looked enquiringly at him.

'Have I got a spot or something?' she asked.

He shook his head. 'No—I was thinking that you have the kind of face a man can look at for ever and never grow tired of.'

She finished her sherry and put the glass down. She sought for something lighthearted to say and came out with: 'You mean nothing startling . . .'

'No, I mean something tranquil and gentle and steadfast—they add up to beauty, Katie.'

She carefully undid the knot of her belt and re-tied it, not looking at him. She must take care not to imagine things—he was being kind as an old friend was kind, nothing else. She said gravely, 'Thank you, Lucius—that's the nicest thing you've ever said to me.' And when he didn't answer: 'Could we go down to dinner? I'm very hungry.'

He agreed at once, looking amused, and all they talked of during the meal was of plans for their return home in a day or two's time. And after their meal they wandered outside and sat down for coffee as they had done before. And just as before they hadn't been there long before the cosy little lady stopped by their table. 'Well, fancy seeing you again!' she declared happily. 'Hasn't it all been exciting? There's been an earthquake, you know . . .'

Lucius smiled down at her. 'Yes, we're just back—we were there.'

Her eyes grew round. 'How very interesting! I should so like to . . .'

Her sister, looming at her elbow, cut her short. 'We shall be late for our meal,' she reminded her severely. She eyed Katrina with sternness. 'It has to be hoped that your experience has had a sobering effect upon your way of life,' she remarked acidly. 'Gallivanting around Europe is no way to behave, and you're old enough to know better.'

Katrina stared at her, round-eyed. It was Lucius who answered, his voice very quiet, but there was a note in it which made the woman draw back a step.

'I think you don't know what you're saying, Miss . . . er . . . This young lady, far from gallivanting round Europe, leads an exemplary life in a small village where she does a great deal of good work. She is, moreover, my future wife. Be good enough to bear that in mind. Good evening.' He turned to smile at the upset face of the woman's sister and sat down again. When they had gone he said: 'Sorry about that, love. Not a nice woman at all. I'm sorry for her sister.'

'Well, she did rather take me by surprise,' Katrina grinned suddenly. 'Thanks for the splendid reference!'

'And every word of it true, Katie. Darling Katie!' He smiled at her and took her hand lying on the table. 'We shall be a very happy couple.'

CHAPTER NINE

KATIE sat and looked at him, searching her head for the right answer and coming up with nothing at all, her heart beating so loud and fast that she felt sure he must hear it. When Lucius said, still smiling: 'You don't believe me, do you?' she shook her head and said with convincing lightness: 'No, of course I don't. I expect you've said that to dozens of girls.'

His grey eyes became cold. He said coolly: 'This is obviously neither the time nor the place.'

'What for?'

'The talk we were going to have. If you remember, we were just embarking upon it when the earthquake started.'

She said urgently: 'Lucius, do we have to have it? I mean, you don't have to explain. I know our engagement is phoney because it seemed the right thing to do at the time, but you must want to be free . . . and you don't have to explain. You can have your ring back and I'll tell everyone that we're not—not compatible or something . . .'

'You think that? You really think that?' His smile mocked her. 'Let me tell you something, darling Katie. We're very compatible; we both love the country, love village life, riding, dogs, cats, organising the village jumble sale, having small dinner parties for our friends . . .'

She interrupted him: 'All right, then I'll think of something else. I'll fall in love with someone else . . .' She stopped, her eyes wide, colour flooding her face. 'Don't think I'm in love with you,' she said fiercely, 'but you know what I mean.'

Lucius was lounging back in his chair, his eyes half closed. 'Yes, I know,' he said placidly. 'Katie, must you delve so deep? Could you not accept things as they are—as they're meant to be? We've been friends for so long that you only see me in that light, don't you? Will you try and think of me as a husband? You do, after all, wear my ring.'

'But that was pretence, so that everyone would think—you did it to scotch Virginia's nonsense.'

'Indeed yes, but that was not the only reason.' Lucius leaned forward and took her hands in his. 'Listen to me, I won't say another word until we get home, but until then will you stop thinking of me as an old friend and think instead of me as a man you've just met who's taken a fancy to you?' He released her hands and lounged back once more. 'We'd better go shopping tomorrow and see what we can find to take back with us, and I must see about the wreckage of the car we hired. Won't it be pleasant to sleep in a bed again?'

Katrina answered him at random. What exactly had he meant? That he had fallen a little in love with her? That marrying her might be convenient to them both? She hoped that it was the former— but he had never made any pretence of being in love with her. There could be a worse fate than marrying someone you had known since childhood, she supposed. You would know each other, faults and all, for a start, but how would she ever go on pretending she was just a good friend when she was head over heels in love with him? She gave up worrying about it and instead discussed the purchase of gifts that they would have to take back with them.

They spent the next day amicably enough, searching out suitable presents, watching the guard outside what had been the Royal Palace, strolling in the Royal Gardens and drinking coffee in the sunshine. And because it was their last night in Athens, they went out to dinner, taking a taxi to one of the restaurants along the coast towards Sounion. They stayed late, driving back after midnight and arranging to meet at the hotel swimming pool in the morning.

There was no one else there when Katrina reached the pool the following morning, only Lucius, tearing up and down its length. She slid in from the shallow end and began a rather sedate progress towards the other end. He passed her several times on the way, calling a cheerful good morning, and presently, after swimming the length of the pool twice, she got out and left him there, calling that she would see him at breakfast.

She dressed without haste, packed her case and went to the sitting room. He was already there, lying back in a chair, his feet on a convenient table, reading a newspaper. 'I've packed,' she told him smugly.

'Clever girl! We don't leave until two o'clock. I thought we might have a last coffee in the square before lunch. Unless you want to go sight seeing.'

She said seriously: 'Haven't we seen everything?' and at his amused look: 'No, I daresay we haven't. But coffee and doing nothing sounds nice.'

They spent a pleasant morning, strolling along wherever the mood took them before going back to the hotel for lunch before they packed their final things and drove to the airport. It seemed a good deal longer than two weeks since they had arrived, but that was because so much had happened. Katrina settled herself into the window seat, fastened her seatbelt and opened the magazine Lucius had bought her. The plane was half empty and they had the first class compartment to themselves. She read the magazine thoroughly from cover to cover, accepted her tea tray and made no attempt to talk to Lucius. She knew that he disliked chatter; besides, he was deep in a dull-looking book about law. There was no cloud today; she watched the fields and towns and villages sliding away beneath them; it was like looking through the wrong end of a telescope, and after a while it got dull. She closed her eyes and pretended sleep until Lucius leaned over to fasten her seatbelt and they landed at Heathrow.

They went through the routine of collecting luggage, passports, Customs, and emerged finally to find that the car was outside. Katrina got in thankfully while Lucius paid off the garage hand who had brought it. It was dark now and cold, and she was glad of her coat and the comfort of the car.

'We'll stop somewhere and eat,' said Lucius, getting in beside her. 'Will there be anyone waiting up at your place?'

'I told Lovelace it would be late evening when we got back and he never goes to bed before eleven o'clock.'

'We'll be home by then.'

There wasn't a great deal of traffic on the roads, and in no time at all they were in Oxford. Lucius stopped at the end of the High Street and ushered her into La Sorbonne, to be greeted by the proprietor and given a table in a corner and the instant attention of the wine waiter. It was nice to sip sherry again, thought Katrina, trying to decide between steak with mushrooms and chicken à la crème; she settled for the steak followed by crêpes Suzette and drank the claret Lucius chose. It was all very cosy and pleasant, with the cold January night shut out securely, and the prospect of sleeping in her own bed.

It was half past eleven as Lucius turned the car into the drive and stopped in front of her own door. There was a light in the hall and Lovelace was there, ushering them inside almost before they could get out of the car.

'Welcome back, Miss Katrina, and you, Mr Lucius. There's coffee and drinks in the sitting room. I'll see to the luggage, sir.'

There was a fire still burning and a tray with the coffee on a small table by it. Katrina shed her coat, tossed her gloves and handbag on to a chair and sat down. 'How nice! Lucius, put your coat on a chair and come by the fire; have some coffee before you go.' She turned to Lovelace as he came into the room with a plate of sandwiches. 'Is everything all right, Lovelace—any news?'

'Nothing that can't wait until tomorrow, Miss Katrina. Miss Virginia and Mr Lovell are back. She telephoned to know when you would be returning.'

'Oh, good. I expect they'll be over tomorrow. Don't stay up, Lovelace, I'll bolt the door. You must be tired. The coffee is lovely.'

Lovelace smiled. 'We've all missed you, Miss Katrina—and I do hear that over at Stockley they are most anxious to see Mr Lucius back home.'

He wished them both goodnight with dignity and went away, leaving them to drink their coffee and eat Mrs Beecham's carefully made sandwiches. With her mouth inelegantly full, Katrina said: 'It was a lovely holiday, Lucius. Thank you very much.'

'But it's nice to be home?'

'Well, yes. But it really was super, and I'll never forget it.'

'Don't tell me you'll remember all the gods and temples and Byzantine churches . . .?'

'Heavens, no—I meant the people we met and the glorious scenery and the villages.' And you, she added silently.

Lucius put down his cup and saucer and stood up. 'Well, I'm going home now. Cobb mustn't be kept up too late, he's getting old. I'll be over tomorrow, sometime.'

Katrina got to her feet and walked with him into the hall and stood there while he put on his coat and went to the door, but he came back again.

'The only thing that I really remember is you,' he told her softly. 'You beat the Greek goddesses into cocked hats.' He bent and kissed her very gently and then again, not gently at all. His goodnight echoed from the door as he closed it behind him.

Katrina stood still, wishing with all her heart that he would come back and kiss her again like that, but he didn't, and presently she bolted the door and went up to bed with Bouncer in close attendance, to lie awake and wonder.

What with the long journey and rather a sleepless night, Katrina didn't look her best in the morning, and to make matters worse Lucius rang to say that he was going up to London and wouldn't be back until the late evening. She spent an hour with Mrs

Beecham in the kitchen, went through her post and, well wrapped up against the cold damp day, took Bouncer for a long walk. When she got back it was to find Virginia sprawled in front of the sitting room fire.

Virginia looked marvellous; tanned and sparkling, dressed unsuitably but glamorously in suede and fur. She eyed Katrina, surprisingly critically. 'Well, you don't show much result from your two weeks in Greece, do you?' was her greeting. 'What on earth have you done to yourself?'

Katrina rang for coffee and sat down by the fire. 'It's cold out,' she said mildly. 'You're looking super, Virginia. Did you have a good honeymoon?'

'Lord, yes—all that sun, and James bought me more clothes than I'll ever wear. I'm on my way to town now to pick up a dress that had to be altered.'

'Back this evening?'

'Oh, yes. Mother-in-law's giving some dreary dinner party we'll have to go to. What did you do in Greece?'

'Looked at ruins.'

'God, how dreary! Where is Lucius?'

'In London for the day.' Katrina got up to pour the coffee. 'You must both come over for dinner soon.'

Virginia took her cup. 'Still wearing the ring, I see. Don't tell me he's serious?' She sounded so astonished that Katrina said rather sharply:

'Well, you were the first to say so, weren't you?' and then, 'Sorry, love, I didn't mean to snap, but I didn't sleep very well, I was too tired.'

Virginia drank her coffee and got up. 'Well, I'm

off. I'm having lunch in town so I can leave before the rush hour. I'll give you a ring.'

She roared away, going much too fast as she always did, and Katrina went back to the fire to drink another cup of coffee before starting on her letter writing.

The grey skies of the morning turned greyer and presently it began to sleet. She had finished her letters by mid-afternoon, wrapped up the book cover she intended to take up to London within the next few days, and was pouring her first cup of tea when she heard the front door opened and light footsteps in the hall. Virginia, unexpectedly back.

'Just in time for tea,' she observed cheerfully. 'What a beastly afternoon! Did you have a good trip?' She turned to take a cup and saucer Lovelace had brought and looked across at her sister.

Virginia had thrown her coat over a chair and curled up in an armchair by the fire. 'I'll have a cup of tea but nothing else. I ought to be home, but I simply had to call in on the way. There's something you ought to know.'

Katrina studied her sister's lovely face: it bore a look of excited anticipation, like a small girl bursting to tell a secret. She smiled. 'Do tell, darling.'

'I was coming out of Harrods and I had to wait in the porch for a bit because it was raining, and who do you think I saw?' And as Katrina didn't speak: 'Lucius—with a girl, a stunning creature. He had an arm round her shoulders and she was looking up at him ...' Virginia smirked: 'You know—all soft and adoring. He stopped a taxi and put her into it and kissed her.' She added: 'He didn't see me.'

Katrina's mouth had gone dry; all the same she managed a perfectly normal voice. 'What of it, love? She's not the first girl he's kissed, and why shouldn't he if he wants to?'

'He is engaged to you, isn't he? Even if the whole thing is phoney—and I bet you cooked it up between you just to spite me—but everyone thinks you're going to get married.' She added huffily: 'You don't have to believe me, of course.'

'Of course I believe you, but why all the fuss?'

Virginia got to her feet. 'I must go home. You're in love with him, aren't you? And I suppose you think I'd not noticed that. Take my advice and do something about it.'

'Why should I?' Katrina managed a cool voice, only faintly interested. 'Give my love to James and his mother, won't you? We must fix a date for dinner one evening.'

Virginia shot her a bad-tempered look and flounced out of the room. Katrina heard her voice in the hall, speaking with unwonted sharpness to Lovelace.

She was half way through her solitary dinner when Lucius arrived. Lovelace followed him in, ready to lay a place at table for him, but he said: 'No, I can't stop, Katie, I'm late back as it is. Have you had a good day?'

She had made up her mind to ignore Virginia's gossip; all the same her voice came out a little stiff. 'Yes, quite busy, really.' She examined the dinner on her plate and avoided his eye. 'What was London like?'

'Horrible! Shall we go riding tomorrow?'

She said a little too quickly: 'Oh, I can't—I've an appointment at the publishers.'

He looked at her. His eyes narrowed. 'Not

wasting much time, are you? Or have you got an unexpected commission?'

'Yes—yes, that's it.' She went on rather feverishly, because she was a poor liar. 'It will be nice to have something to do.'

Lucius strolled to the door. 'No, don't get up, I'll see myself out.' He paused, his hand on the door handle. 'Have you seen Virginia?'

'She came over this morning and—and she popped in on her way home early this evening.' She looked quickly at him and away again. 'She looks terrific.'

Lucius didn't say anything, only nodded to her as he went.

Katrina would have to go up to London now, she decided. It was bad enough having to lie like that, the least she could do was to turn it into some kind of truth. And probably there would be some work waiting for her.

She left early and when she got to London went straight to the publishers, glad to find that there was in fact another book jacket for her to design. Now if Lucius wanted concrete evidence of her visit, she could produce it. Not that he would ask. For as long as she could remember he had never once doubted her word. She had coffee with the publisher, agreed on a delivery date, and went back to her car. Since she was in town she might as well have lunch and look for a pair of shoes to replace the pair she had ruined in Greece. She parked the car, had an early lunch at a small restaurant close by Old Bond Street, and set off to scrutinize the shoe shops. She found what she wanted without much trouble, and started back towards the car, trying to decide if she should go home at once or stay another hour or so, have tea and get home in the evening. She was standing on the corner of Conduit Street and Bond Street waiting to cross the road when she saw Lucius. He was coming out of the Westbury Hotel and hanging on his arm was a slim fair-haired girl. They walked away from her, along Conduit Street, deep in talk.

Katrina stood staring after them until an impatient woman behind her gave her a shove so that she had to cross the street. But there she stopped again, oblivious of people rushing past her, giving her irritable glances. Lucius and his companion were almost out of sight, but they were standing still now, still talking, and Lucius's arm was around the girl's shoulders. Katrina drew a long breath and turned into Bond Street, back towards the car. She very much wanted to run after them and ask who the girl was and why they were there, together, and although her feet took her away from them at every step, her mind was still with them. It stayed that way as she drove back to Tew, put the car away, pushed food around her plate at dinner and then went to sit by the fire with Bouncer. Virginia had been right, after all. The small vague hope that Lucius was beginning to fall just a little in love with her, born of his kiss and the things he had said when he had brought her home two days ago, withered slowly. She must make an end of the business, give him back his ring and let the gossip have its head for a few days. She supposed she would have to give some reason, however paltry, so it could be done in a friendly way. They had always been friends, she thought wistfully, so deep in thought that she didn't hear Lucius's quiet entry and quieter voice in the hall.

He was in the room, walking towards her before she knew that he was there.

His 'Hullo' was exactly as usual, and he was smiling. But then he stopped, his eyes on her face. 'What's the matter?' he asked sharply.

Katrina said, not mincing her words: 'I was in London today. I saw you there; you were with a girl—it was outside the Westbury. When Virginia came yesterday she told me she'd seen you with her and I—I thought she was just being—well, trying to make trouble and I told her I didn't believe her . . .'

His eyes were cold, his voice colder. 'And you believe her now?'

'Well, I saw you!' Her voice, despite her best efforts, had become a little shrill.

'And what does that prove?' He asked the question silkily, but she ignored the mockery in his face and went on quickly: 'You said you'd decided to—to marry, that this engagement of ours was just to put an end to Virginia's silly tale, and it's ridiculous to go on like this, pretending.' She gulped back threatening tears. 'Here's your ring, thank you for letting me wear it. I'll tell everyone I've changed my mind.'

She held it out and he took it without a word, and when she peeped at his face she saw that he was very angry indeed. He had a nasty temper which he had learned to hide under an icy manner which was far worse than an explosion of rage, but that didn't worry her overmuch, she had known him too long. She made one last effort. 'We'll still be friends?'

He was leaning against a table, tossing the ring up and down with one hand. 'What makes you think that, my dear?'

He had gone before she could reply.

Katrina went to bed after that and had a good cry in her room, sniffing and spluttering in a manner reminiscent of her childhood. But she felt a little better, and presently, worn out with unhappiness, she slept.

Half way through the next morning she remembered that old Lady Ryder was giving what she called an evening party that night. Guests were bidden for six o'clock and were expected to leave within a couple of hours. She had already accepted the invitation and Lucius would naturally be going. It was hardly an ideal place in which to let it be known that their engagement had come unstuck; it might be better if they behaved towards each other as they normally did and said nothing, especially as Virginia and James would be there. She decided to go late and leave early—a headache or toothache, or better still, she'd get Lovelace to telephone and ask her to go back home; she need not give a reason. Satisfied with this plan and solution to a ticklish situation, she repaired to her room and inspected her wardrobe. The brown velvet suit, she decided, and her amber beads.

She could see the Bentley outside Stockley house as she walked Bouncer later that afternoon, but she didn't linger to watch if Lucius was going anywhere. She got back after a lengthy walk, had a cup of tea and went upstairs to change. She didn't hurry, and Lovelace, a stickler for punctuality, gave her a reproving look as she went out to the car, and then one of surprise as she instructed him to telephone her in an hour's time at Lady Ryder's. 'Very good, Miss Katrina,' he said, allowing the faintest curiosity to show.

'I particularly want to leave before everyone else, Lovelace, so don't forget, will you?'

Lady Ryder's drawing room was nicely full as she went in and she saw Virginia and James almost at once. Lady Ryder, after urging her to come to tea soon and tell her all about Greece, left her to find her way from one group of friends to the next. She had just left Virginia and James and settled to a staid conversation with Mrs Moffat when Lucius came in. The girl Katrina had seen in London was with him and Katrina was astonished to see Lady Ryder kiss her with the easy familiarity of an old friend before lifting her face for Lucius's kiss.

Katrina, nodding and smiling vaguely at Mrs Moffat's steady flow of talk, kept her eyes glued on the three of them, and when Lucius looked up and stared back at her, she was quite unable to look away.

'There's Lucius,' declared Mrs Moffat, a woman guaranteed to state the obvious at all times. 'And who is the pretty girl with him? She's coming over here. An old friend, my dear?'

A deadly enemy, thought Katrina, and pasted a smile on her white face.

The girl stopped in front of her, smiled at Mrs Moffat and turned to Katrina. 'You haven't changed a bit, Katie,' she declared. 'Don't you remember me? Cousin Mary, who climbed trees with you and Lucius in the summer holidays?'

Katrina's lovely eyes opened wide and her jaw dropped. 'Good lord, Mary! Aren't you in Canada?'

Mary laughed. 'No, ducky—here. My dear husband is still there, but he's being transferred in a couple of weeks and he sent me on ahead to find somewhere to live. I've been in town for two days looking for a house or flat. Thank heaven Lucius answered my cries for help and has been aiding me.'

She sipped her drink and made a small face. 'I hear Virginia's married. I must wish her happy, I suppose. Just as spoilt as she always was? When are you and Lucius going to get married? I asked him this evening when he met me at Oxford, but he's being very poker-faced. Is it a secret?' She glanced at Katrina's left hand. 'Where's the famous family sapphire?' Her eyes flew to Katrina's face. 'What have you done to your finger?'

'Oh, I burnt it; not badly, but I couldn't bear the ring on it.' Katrina uttered the fib awkwardly and blushed guiltily. 'Have you found somewhere to live?'

'Yes, thank heaven—Lucius met me yesterday again and we signed the lease, or at least I did, with him breathing cousinly advice down my neck, and then we celebrated over lunch at the Westbury. I phoned Laurie too and he's delighted; he'll be here in a week. I miss him.' Mary grinned. 'That's not bad after five years, is it? I'll tell you something else—I'm having a baby in July.'

'That's lovely! Oh, Mary, it's super to see you again. You'll have to come and stay with me . . .'

'With you both,' corrected Mary. 'Here's Lucius, beating his way to you. What a crowd!'

Katrina had been dreading meeting him face to face, but she need not have worried; his, 'Hullo, Katie', was exactly right, pleasantly affectionate. He smiled too, only his eyes were cold as he looked down at her. 'Cut your finger?' he asked casually, and watched as the colour washed over her face once more.

'Burnt—not badly, though.' She managed a

smile for Mary's benefit. 'It'll be all right tomorrow.'

She tried to think of something to say. Lucius wasn't going to help and Mary was looking at her with a faint amused smile. Oh, God, send that message from Lovelace, prayed Katrina silently, and let out an audible sigh of relief when Lady Ryder came towards her. 'My dear, there's a message from your butler, he asks that you should go back—nothing catastrophic, he says, but only you can deal with it.'

Katrina's face wore the expression of someone who had just been offered a reprieve under the very shadow of the scaffold. 'Oh, how tiresome,' she declared, and the relief in her voice was so marked that Lucius, watching her face with eyes alight with amusement, said dryly: 'I'll drive you if you like, Katie?'

'No—oh no, thanks. It—I don't expect it's anything much. I'll see you ... Mary, give me a ring soon, will you? It's been lovely ...'

She said goodbye to Lady Ryder and slipped away. Thank heaven that was over, and she considered that she'd managed rather well. It had been pure inspiration putting a plaster round her finger. As she drove she reviewed the days ahead. There were one or two dinner parties to which naturally enough Lucius had been invited too; she would have to have 'flu or something for a few days, and by then he wouldn't be angry any more and she would apologise ... She drew up before her door, but she didn't get out of the car. There was no help for it, she would have to tell him the truth and he could make what he liked of it. The tiny hope that perhaps he loved her just a little was doused by the memory of his cold eyes. She got out of the car, then got in again and drove it to the garage and walked slowly back to the house.

She had supper on a tray, took Bouncer for a quick walk in the gardens and then went to bed to spend most of the night rehearsing what she would say to Lucius. By now she was concerned only with telling him everything. He would have to sort out the muddle afterwards. She had no doubts that he would be able to do that; he had always dealt with her problems for her.

She got up late, heavy-eyed and looking rather pale, plain and quite unable to face breakfast, took Bouncer for a walk and then on impulse, cast an anorak over her sweater and skirt and walked down the drive, along the lane and in through the open gates of Stockley House. Cobb was crossing the hall as she mounted the steps, and he opened the door to her and she said rather wildly: 'Don't bother to say I'm here, I'll go in.'

Lucius would be in his study. Katrina crossed the hall with Cobb tutting behind her, gave a perfunctory knock on the door and opened it. Lucius was sitting at his desk and his farm manager was sitting opposite him. He looked up as she went in and stopped short just inside the door.

'I'm sorry—I didn't know that there was someone with you.' She sounded despairing.

Lucius had got to his feet. 'Hullo, Katie,' he said gently. 'Don't go.' He handed his manager some papers. 'See about those repairs, Tim, and check the price of that feed we ordered. We'll leave the rest until tomorrow morning.'

When they were alone, he said: 'I'm listening, Katie. Do you want to sit down?'

'No.' At the sight of him all her prepared

speeches flew out of her head. 'Lucius, I didn't know it was Mary. I—I thought it was a girl—the girl you're going to marry. I'm truly sorry for being so beastly and not giving you a chance to say anything, but it wouldn't have mattered, would it? Only I won't go on like this any longer; it's all such a muddle.' She drew a breath. 'I haven't burnt my finger,' she added, as though that were important. 'And what I really came to say was that I've been in love with you for quite some time, which makes it all very awkward.' She wasn't looking at him any more, but it was a relief to spill everything out, just as she had done since she was a little girl. 'I thought if I went away for a bit—there's Aunt Edna in Scotland . . .' She stopped because Lucius was laughing.

'My darling girl!' He came round the desk and put his arms around her. 'My dear, darling girl, of all the nonsense—the only sensible thing you've said is that you love me, and my goodness, I was beginning to think you'd never admit it! Just cast your muddled mind back, my love. The reason I went around with Virginia was so that I could see more of you; the reason I suggested we became engaged to confound all her silly tales was because it seemed a heavensent opportunity to get you into the right frame of mind to fall in love with me. I thought I was succeeding in Greece, too.'

He lifted her hand and pulled the plaster off her finger and took the ring out of a pocket and slipped it back on. 'You are truly delightful, and I love you, my darling. I think I've loved you since you were a little girl, and I've watched you grow into a lovely woman . . .'

'Lovely? asked Katrina, amazed.

'Lovely.' He bent to kiss her. Presently he said:

'I've got a special licence in my pocket, so we can be married when we like. You shall wear that pink thing and the hat with roses—you looked beautiful . . .'

She smiled at him. 'Did I? You said "Roses and Champagne." '

Lucius kissed her again. 'I'm a romantic man at heart,' he told her.

Harlequin® Plus

A WORD ABOUT THE AUTHOR

Betty Neels, whose first Harlequin was published in 1970, is well-known for her stories set in the Netherlands. This is not surprising. Betty is married to a Dutchman, and she spent the first twelve years of her marriage in Holland. Today she and her husband, Johannes, return there as often as three times a year.

As Betty travels, always visiting some fresh spot in Holland, she chooses houses, streets and villages to use in her books; whenever possible she will venture inside privately owned buildings. "And of course," she laughs, "I tend to go through life eavesdropping on conversations in buses and trains and shops." An excellent way, we think, to garner ideas for romance novels.

Betty Neels is a retired nurse. Today she and Johannes make their home in a small three-hundred-year-old stone cottage in England's West Country, where, she says, life moves along at a pleasantly unhurried pace.

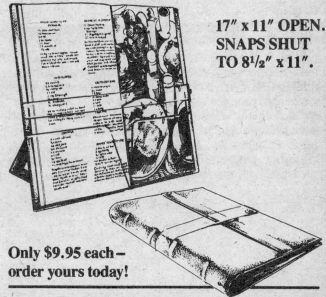

Enter a uniquely exciting new world with

Harlequin American Romance ™·

Harlequin American Romances are the first romances to explore today's love relationships. These compelling novels reach into the hearts and minds of women across America... probing the most intimate moments of romance, love and desire.

You'll follow romantic heroines and irresistible men as they boldly face confusing choices. Career first, love later? Love without marriage? Long-distance relationships? All the experiences that make love real are captured in the tender, loving pages of **Harlequin American Romances.**

What makes American women so different when it comes to love? Find out with **Harlequin American Romance!**

Send for your introductory FREE book now!

Get this book FREE!

Mail to:

Harlequin Reader Service

In the U.S.
2504 West Southern Avenue
Tempe, AZ 85282

In Canada
649 Ontario Street
Stratford, Ontario N5A 6W2

YES! I want to be one of the first to discover **Harlequin American Romance.** Send me FREE and without obligation *Twice in a Lifetime.* If you do not hear from me after I have examined my FREE book, please send me the 4 new **Harlequin American Romances** each month as soon as they come off the presses. I understand that I will be billed only $2.25 for each book (total $9.00). There are no shipping or handling charges. There is no minimum number of books that I have to purchase. In fact, I may cancel this arrangement at any time. *Twice in a Lifetime* is mine to keep as a FREE gift, even if I do not buy any additional books.

Name	(please print)

Address	Apt. no.

City	State/Prov.	Zip/Postal Code

Signature (If under 18, parent or guardian must sign.)